OH HENRY!

OH HENRY!

by

Sol Weinstein & Howard Albrecht

Combustoica
a prose project of About Comics - Camarillo, California

IN MEMORIAM
Dora Kaplan, a beloved aunt
Abel Green, of *Variety*
Jack E. Leonard

OH HENRY!
by Sol Weinstein & Howard Albrecht

2014 edition

Published by Combustoica, a prose project of About Comics.
WWW.COMBUSTOICA.COM

Rights inquiries? *rights@AboutComics.com*

DEDICATIONS

ELLIE WEINSTEIN and BERNICE ALBRECHT
Wondrous wives.

DAVID and JUDEE WEINSTEIN; SHELLEE and RICHARD ALBRECHT
Peerless progeny.

SAM and CHAI SOORA WEINSTEIN and ADA ALBRECHT
May they shepp naches from their sons' monumental literature.

SHEPP NACHES
The wrangler of the old Bar Kochba Ranch, Tel-Aviv.

DR. and MRS. HOWARD S. FRIEDMAN and BELKE, SETH and JOEL.

JANET, JERI and STEVEN ALBRECHT, TEDDY and EDDY ALBRECHT, STUART and
PRISCILLA ALBRECHT, JOE and HANNA FREEDLAND, JOE and CYLVIA ALDERMAN,
STEVE and JANET LEVINSON.

HARRY and BESS EISNER, MR. and MRS. STAN EISNER, SAM and MARY GENTILE.

BILL (MR. LA.) KENNEDY and his EVE Of the Los Angeles *Herald-Examiner.*

RONN OWENS
Of WCAU, WKAT, WERE and now WJW, Cleveland. A fine two-way radio talk
host who is moving ever closer to his goal… back to WCAU.

LES and GAIL ROBERTS Of Sherman Oaks, Calif.

SAUL and JULIE ILSON and ERNEST and VERONICA CHAMBERS

SHELDON KELLER
Who traveled to Tibet, looked into the heart of a lotus and found a one-
liner. He then sold his guru to the New York Knicks.

(COMMERCIAL BREAK NUMBER ONE: Read *The Oddfather,* two hours of Pinnacle
Books* paperback hilarity by Sol Weinstein and Howards Albrecht, a saga of
the true Mafia and a documentary on the various uses of cement. Now, back
to the dedications…)

DICK WEST
Of United Press International, who will have trouble following this novel
of political espionage because he thinks a double agent is one who writes
insurance for both Prudential and Metropolitan.

NORTON MOCKRIDGE
Nifty columnist, lover of shtick.

EARL WILSON
If it happened on Broadway he knows about it because he did it.

SAUL BASS
Of Woodland Hills, Calif., true Renaissance man, aerospace executive, font
of wisdom, freelance plumber. With thanks for the frequent technological
data he has supplied that has afforded our books a badly needed touch of
authenticity. And to GRACE, RONNIE, SUE and JEFF.

IRV, MALGERT, KIVA, RACHEL and ELISA COHEN

ROSE (SAM) DeWOLF
Of *The Philadelphia Bulletin,* superchick. And her BERNIE INGSTER.

JACK McKINNEY, LARRY FIELDS, CHARLES PETZOLD and TOM ¥ FOX
Of The Philadelphia Daily News.

LEON BROWN
Of The Philadelphia Jewish Exponent.

MEL KNOEPP
Of KFMB-TV, San Diego.

DALE SCHWARTZ and JACK WHITE
Of KGTV-10, San Diego.

SUSAN FARRELL
Of CABLE-7 TV, San Diego.

RED ROWE
Of KCST-TV, San Diego. What la a Red Rowe? A string of Communist
embassies on Parle Avenue? A command to the Harvard racing shell? Shad
dipped In vermilion? There is a vast field for humor here.

BILL GORDON
Of KSDO, San Diego. Jogger, nutritionist, wit, raconteur, defiler of the
guitar.

JERRY IZENBERG and DEAN LONG
Of KITT, San Diego.

IRWIN ZUCKER and NANCY SAYLES JACK MOORE
Of KOGO, San Diego.

(COMMERCIAL BREAK NUMBER TWO: You have the effrontery to admit you haven't
read *Jonathan Segal Chicken,* the story of a chicken who dares to fly,
by Sol Weinstein and Howard Albrecht In Pinnacle Books paperback? Your
passport, please. Do you have relatives In Plainfield, New Jersey?)

LANE and ELAINE WOLMAN, HARVEY and BEV MOLL, CELIA SHAPIRO, CELIA CANTOR,
NELSON TYLER, SUSAN BANES, LILA GARRETT, MORT LACHMAN, LYNN ROTH, MILLY
SCHOENBAUM, MEL and EDITH TOLKIN, JOHN and JANET MARGUSEE.

BECKY INMAN

DORIS DAY, GODFREY CAMBRIDGE, BUDDY HACKETT, MILTON BERLE, JOEY and
SYLVIA BISHOP, ALLAN and WANDA DRAKE, LOUIE and ANITA NYE, SID and VANDA
GOULD, MARTY ALLEN, CARL and ESTELLE REINER, BARRY SHEAR, MEL FRANK, NOR-
MAN PANAMA, TONY WEBSTER MIMI HINES, DAVID STEINBERG, JERRY HELLER BTTSY,
JAMIE and CASEY KELLER TIMMIE (OH YEAH!) ROGERS and BARBARA, LOU MARSH
and TONY ADAMS.

UNCLB H. J. SHERMAN, TANTEH CLARA SHERMAN, JOSH SHERMAN, JAKE and DORIS
SHERMAN, DR YEHUDA SHERMAN, JACK and MARY SHERMAN, PHYLLIS SHERMAN.

TONY CURTIS, PAT HENRY, JAN MURRAY, MORTY GUNTY, MARTY PASETTA, HAL and
ELLIB ROSS, RICHARD ROTH, GEORGE DISKANT, MACK GRAY, HENRY (RED) MANDEL,
ANNE MENNA.

BOB WYNN, BOB BOOKER and GEORGE FOSTER; BETTY JANE YORK and STEFANIE
SHULMAN
Of The NBC FOLLIES.

ANDY GRIFFITH, SAMMY DAVIS JR., MICKY ROONEY, CONNIE STEVENS, JOHN
DAVIDSON.

LOU JACOBI, ARI and SHULAMTTH RUTKOFF, MOLLY LEVINE, GLORIA WOLFORD,
MICHAEL end CAROLINB ELIAS, GORDON and LYN FARR ARNOLD KANE, JERRY
SCHOENBAUM, DELLA WASSERMAN, BETH UFFNER MORTY and BETTY WEST, PAUL WAYNE
MARVIN and EVELYN WINKLER and ROMAIN, who didn't lettuce.

(COMMERCIAL BREAK NUMBER THREE: For succulent Sashimi, tasty teriyaki
and a promise never again to establish a Greater East Asia Co-Prosperity
Sphere, it's the TEMPURA INN at Canoga and DeSoto, Canoga Park, Calif.)

BOB and SABRINA SCHILLER, BOB and EILEEN WEISKOPF, MARILYN CUNNINGHAM, and
AGNES, BEA and MARGE at Schwab's, Beverly Hills.

HELEN
Of Nate N' Al's, Beverly Hills, the "Lox Box."

ART HOPPE

CAROL AXE, BOBBI WEINER, LYNN SHANKS, LOIS and CLAUDIA SLOAN, MORRIS and
ELENA DIAMOND, DR. ERNIE and EUNICE WHITE, VICKI CHRISTOPHER, DR. JEROME
BRISKIN, EDIE GLADSTONE, WILLIE and BESS DIAMOND, THEBE and COOKIE DRAZIN.

HY and KITTY BERKOWITZ, ELLIOT ALEXANDER, BONNY and MYLES GOLDBERG, JOE
and BARBARA GARRAN. BALL and BETTY HANSEN, SUZANNE HILTON, TONY HANDLER,
STANLEY HILTZIK, JUDY ACKERMAN, CLAUDIA ANDERSON, USA MEDFORD, BOB and
PAULETTE LEIBOWTTZ, CHARLES and JOYCE LEIBLER, JIM LOREN, LEE LOEB, SUE
MARTIN, GERRI NELSON, LEE and LOIS POLK, JIMMY RETY, JANNETTE KATZ, IDELL
RUBIN and LARRY SLOAN.

DAVE and BARBARA TTDUS, JACK and SOPHIE ROSENBERG, JACK and FRANCES ROSENBERG, TANIA ©ROSSINGER, NOEL BLANC, NORMAN SHAVIN, MAX YOUNG, GEORGE COHEN, TED PROBER, TOM DUNPHY, LARRY and CAROL ALEXANDER, MARC B. and LORELEI RAY, ADELE GORDON LEON.

JACKIE KANNON
The Ratflnk Room will rise again!

FERN FIELD, CHUCK LICHTER, ELMER KOGLIN, ANITA ALTMAN, MARVIN and CHARLOTTE ZIPORYN, DON BARNETT, WALT and MATH MYERS, ANN ROSSER, WALT CANTER, MIKE and MARILYN ROSENFELD, SIEVE SCHENKEL, MENDY, WILLIE and DAVE KRAVTTZ, STAN and MINDY LEDEXMAN, MARGE and MARIO PASCUCCL BEN MELZER, LIPPY and SYLVIA EISNER and JACK CURTIS of The Latin Casino, Cherry Hill, NJ.

(COMMERCIAL BREAK NUMBER FOUR: In Washington, D.C., to testify? Then catch Mark Russell, the Washington Wit, at the Shoreham Hotel. A brilliant topical humorist. Now, back to the dedications…)

EDWARD D. BROWN

HARRY HARRIS
TV expert of the Philadelphia Inquirer.

JACK HELSEL and MARCIAROSE
Of KYW-TV, Philadelphia.

GARY OWENS of KMPC, Los Angeles, a man who serves Egg McMuffin on the rocks at his glittering Hollywood parties attended by All (Katz) and Rock (Igneous)… and his faithless engineer, WAYNE DuBOIS, and his KMPC cohorts: DICK WHTTTTNGHILL, who sounds like he works In the nude; GEOFF EDWARDS, the Lone Ranger of the Bobby Darin Show and a man who injects himself with 20 oo. of cheerfulness every morning; WINK MARTINDALE, teeth *on* parade; CLARK RACE, a credit to his, etc., dear KATHY GORI, Night Owlets, and DONN REED.

LOHMAN and BARKLEY, of KFI, Los Angeles, two mouths in motion. And their KFI cohorts: JERRY BISHOP, who placed an excellent 23rd In the Ed Sullivan impression derby; HILLY ROSE, with thanks; ROBERT Q. LEWIS; RON McCOY; Rolls Royce-smooth PAUL COMPTON, and MARGO DILLON.

SWEET DICK WHITTINGTON, of KGIL, Los Angeles, polluting the San Fernando Valley with his pernicious doctrines of truth and fair play, a fine, pure radio man, hair stylist and West Coast representative for Baggies, and Ms KGIL cohorts: CHUCK SOUTHCOTT, LARRY (MOTHER) VAN NUYS, TOM (THE AFFAIR) BROWN, SCOTT O'NEIL, BILL SMITH, KEN GRIFFIN, and TOM KRATOCHVIL.

COUSIN DAVE NEAL GOMBERG
Of KYW-TV, Philadelphia, the newsman who uncovered the direct link between Mayor Frank Rizzo and a plate of lasagna.

KEN MINYARD
Of KABC, Lot Anselea, a talented two-way radio talk host "Our guest today will be Marcel Maroeau who will thrill my listeners with 15 minutes of superlative pantomime."

(COMMERCIAL BREAK NUMBER FIVE: In the Miami area to get away from testifying In Washington? Then look through the Herald, News or Sun to see if Paul Gray, premier comedian. Is doing a club date at a Beach hotel. That's Paul Gray, "fun with degeneracy." Now, back to the dedications…)

SAMMY and MITZI SHORE Of the Comedy Store, Hollywood.

ROCCO URBISCI, STAN HARRIS, MARTY RAOAWAY, ARTIE PHILLIPS, MILT ROSEN, SAM and PEGGY RUDOFKER, RON FRIEDMAN, MICKEY ROSS and unstoppable JAY BURTON.

ARMY ARCHERD
Of Daily Variety

HANK GRANT, SUE CAMERON and MARK TAN
Of The Hollywood Reporter.

BILL LINK and DICK LEVINSON Two top guys.

ELIN BELSKY JOE GAZIN
Of KGOB, Thousand Oaks, Calif.

EMIL (THE BULL) SLABODA, STEVE (DUFFY) MERVISH
And all the lads and lattices at The Trentonian, Trenton, N.J., where Sol
Weinstein broke in as a fighting newspaperman with such eye-popping scoops
as: "The West Windsor PTA will meet at 8 P.M. Tuesday in the municipal
hall. A baked Democrat will be served."

HOWIE TEDDER and DAVE BITTAN
Of The Trenton, N.J., Times.

JUDGE PHILLIP FORMAN and SAM RABINOWITZ

E. WILLIAM MANDEL, ARNE SULTAN, JERRY GAGHAN, JACK and SYLVIA YURMAN,
MICKEY WERSH, IRVINO SHURACK, MEL CHINSKEY, SAM AROUESTY, LARRY and SYD
BERNER, ARNOLD BOOKBINDER, NORMAN FRANK, JOE FUTTERMAN, BARRY GERTLER,
WALT GOLDBERG, PAUL HERSHFIELD, LEW HORWITZ, SAUL and SANDY JACOBS, DAVID
and JANINB JACOBY, and GEORGE, ZELLA, GARY and BONNIE FITLEBERG.

DR. STANLEY KATZ
Of Philadelphia.

RABBI WILLIAM FIERVERKER
Of Congregation Beth El, Levittown, Pa.

RABBI BENJAMIN SINCOFF

RABBIS HARRIS H. HIRSCHBERG and STEVE JACOBS
Of Temple Judea, Tarzana, Calif.

RABBI MELVIN GOLD STINE and CANTOR ROBERT TAFF
Of Temple Aliyah, Woodland Hills, Calif.

BERNIE HERMAN
Of WKBS-TV, Philadelphia.

BILL CORSAIR
The late-night hangnail at WCAU Radio, Philadelphia… and JOHN O. DOWNEY;
JACK CLEMENTS; JOEL A. SPIVAK, nasality in the morning; DOM QUINN; ED
HARVEY; JOHN MARION; AUSTIN CULMER; KATHY QUAID; BELLE SCHUMAN; BILL
HART; JACK JONES, and my man, AL JULIUS, master of anything he does.

ANDY MUSSER
Of CBS Sports, N.Y.C.

JESS CAIN
Of WHDH, Boston, and LENNY MEYERS.

DANNY SIMON
Who is mentally rewriting and punching up these dedications even as he
reads them.

HERB RAU

HERB KELLY

AUSTIN and IRMA KALISH

CRISWELL
"I predict that 78,000 tse-tse flies will attack the No-Doz factory…"

BILL BIRCHER
Of WTMR Camden, NJ.

RIP TAYLOR

BOBBY DARIN, DICK BAKALYAN, GORDON WILES, CHARLIE ISAACS, ALAN THICKE,
SIDNEY MILLER, NEAL MARSHALL, TOMMY AMATO, FRANK GERTZ, EDDIE KARAM, BELL
HARGATE, JIMMY JOYCE, ANITA (YUM YUM) MANN, CAROUANE RAPP, JANE TAYLOR,
JUDI BROWN, BOBBY ROZARIO.
Of The Bobby Darin Show.

STEVE LANDESBERG
A magnificent young comedian.
MARILYN SILVERBERG, SUZIE STANFORD, BERNIE BRILLSTEIN, JOB BIGELOW, JANIE
BELL, DEBBIE MILLER RUTH BUZZI and BILL KEKO, MEL CARTER ZELDA SANDS,
JAIME CAESAR BOBBI RIPLEY.

ALAN KING

JIM MULLIGAN, MAURICE DUKE, BILLY HOLMS, LARRY JONAS, MARY ANN FREY, LIL
BALLONOFF, IMO MISTRETTA, KATHI BENSON, DAVE LeVEQUE, and DR. MICHAEL
DEAN.

MICHELLE FRANK

BILL LEWIS, BOBBY GORDON, JOAN MAHER and AUSTIN MACK.

HY and MARILYN GARDNER

IRWIN LIEBERMAN
Of NOSH-O-RAMA, Woodland Hills, Calif., "the dell of the Valley."

LARRY GROSSMAN
Of C.M.A.

(COMMERCIAL BREAK NUMBER SIX: If you've fled Miami to escape the
Washington grand jury, then rendezvous with us at ANNA'S, a splendid
Italian restaurant on Pico Blvd. in West Los Angeles… moderate prices,
groovy essen, quiet and homey.)

KENNY SOLMS and GAIL PARENT, BERNIE ROTHMAN, HUGH WEDLOCK, CAROL
WORTHINGTON, GEORGE YANOK, SHARON MILLER, SIDNEY REZNICK, WALLY and
AUSTINE WARREN, MICKEY DANER, ALAN HARRIS, ROBERT PINCUS, GWENDA TALENS,
LENNIE ROTNOFSKY, DR SEYMOUR and RUTHE LEDIS, TED and SYBIL OOOPER, LINDA
LATZ, YOUIE and CHARLOTTE CAPILUPI, GERRY and SELMA GOULD, LOU and RUTH
DELIN, ALLEN and RACHEL DELIN, MILTON and EVE LEVINE, BOBBY and MONA
COURTNEY, HARVEY and HARRIET BLATT, LOUIS CRAVTTZ, BILL and LIL HOLSTEIN,
ARNIE and CAROL BERNSTEIN, SAM and CEIL CRAVITT, DR. LEWIS and MARGIE
HIRSH, and NORMA NANNINI of Variety.

BILL GAINES, AL FELDSTEIN and NICK MEGLIN
Of Mad Magazine.

SAM JACOBS
Of American-Jewish Life, Trenton, NJ.

CLARENCE PETERSEN
Of The Chicago Tribune, with thanks.

LARRY DeVINE and BOB TALBERT
Of The Detroit Free Press.

HARRY BOTOFF, NEIL LEVENSON, IRWIN and HERB SPIEGEL, BERNIE GOLDBERG,
JUDGE MARK LITOWITZ, JULIUS (YUDEL) KAPLAN, ISRAEL (COKE) RUBIN, ART
AZARCHI, CHARLES TRESKY and DAVE HORWITZ.
Of WCAM, Camden, N.J.

HY STEIRMAN

FORREST DUKE
Of The Las Vegas Review-Joumal

JOE DELANEY
Of The Las Vegas Sun

FRAN WHITEMAN
Of Valley View, Canoga Park, Calif.

GENE FERRET, BIG JOHN RAPPAPORT, RON POLAO, HORACE GREELY McNAB, MRS.
JERRY L. WAYMAN, IRVING STEIN, BEN STEIN and ED HANLEY.

THE AL CARMONA AGENCY
Of Encino, Calif.

BERT PECK
Of The Encino Book Shop.

THOMAS A. CIOFALO
Of Warner Paperback Library, N.Y.C.

MILLIE MARMUR
of Simon & Schuster.

THE GANG AT
The Camden, N.J., *Courier-Post*

LAURA and ROGER YAGER

JAMES J. SHAPIRO
Of Simplicity Patterns.

YVONNE WILDER

ROBERT and VICKI LANE

NAT and MONICA SCHWARTZ

DR. BERNARD and RHODA AMSTER

WALT and LILLIAN LAMOND

JAY STEVENS
Of WGBS, Miami

BOB and ADELE HOGAN

AL and FRANCES HEYMAN

JOEY ADAMS
Of WEVB, N.Y.C.

JOE FRANKLIN
Of WOR, N.Y.C.

SANDY OPPENHEIMER, BEN BOROWSKY and MIKE RENSHAW
Of The Bodes County & Burlington County Courier-Times.

WALLY PHILLIPS
Of WGN, Chicago. Big Wally they call him because he's apt to pop out of
any wall. And MARILYN MILLER.

IRV KUPCINET
Of Kup's Show, WMAQ-TV, Chicago.

RAY BARNETT
Of KNX, Los Angeles.

CHARLIE PARKER and WALTER DIBBLE
Of WDRC, Hartford, Conn.

JOHN BIRCHARD
Of WELI, New Haven.

BILL SMITH
Of WKAT, Miami; the only radio station ever to check into a motel under
an assumed name.

JACK WHEELER
Of KDKA, Pittsburgh, amplified hominy grits. Hominy grits? How do we know
hominy grits? 40… 50… 60 tops…

J.P. McCarthy
Of WJR, Detroit.

JOHN HUDDY
Of The Miami Herald.

JERRY WILLIAMS and LARRY GLICK
Of WBZ, Boston.

JIM KLASH
Of WDAS, Philadelphia.
ELAINE STEIN
Of WCBM, Baltimore.

HERB KENNY
Of The Boston Globe.

JOSEPH G. WEISBERG

Of The Jewish Advocate, Boston, a prince of a blintz.

DR. RALPH COGAN, DR. MAXWELL SAUNDERS, DR. DONALD W. LUBER, DR. STANLEY
C. ROSS, DR. GERALD ZIMMERMAN, DR. ROBERT CARLTON, DR. ROBERT A. GRANT,
DR. DENNIS PERLOW, and DR. ELLIOT HARRIS, mind blower.

JOHN GEARY, JACK NEBO, LARRY KATES, RUTH BARRY, LINDA WILLIAMS and EVELYN
CROCE
Of THE COMMUNITY CENTER PHYSICAL THERAPY SERVICE, Canoga Park, Calif.

DEE BLUEMEL, DON VAN ATTA, SHIRLEY RITTER, JACK FINSTON, HANK and BARBARA
KATES, GENE and AUDREY RODGERS, IRV and BEVERLY PEDOWITZ, KIRK NUROCK, MEL
and MARGE LIFSON, TOM and BETTY BRENEMAN, GEORGE and KARIN BREITWIESER,
RICHARD and MARILYN READ, ALICE HELGESON, MARV and NORMA GATES, SYLVIA
WEINSTOCK, BOB and SHIRLEY ROBERTS, BOB and JOAN STULMAN, LARRY and BETTY
WAGREICH, EDDIE and ALICE GREENBERG, ARNIE and SANDRA SIMON, SOL, HELEN
and HANNAH ROTNOFSKY, ROSE and ELYSB RUDOW, RICHARD and RICKI RUDOW, BENNY
and JENNIE LINDENBAUM, EVA, SID and CHARLOTTE LINDENBAUM, CHARLES and
BELLA GREENBERG, CY and CLAIRE NEIBURG, SID and ESTELLE LUTZKER.

LEN and NORA FISCHMAN SANDY BARNETT CLYDE and BARBARA LEIB PHYLLIS
FISCHMAN

(COMMERCIAL BREAK NUMBER SEVEN: Send a few dollars to the Israeli
Emergency Fund.)

MARV and PHYLLIS HABAS

JOHN TOMARYN
Of John's Arco Station, 22375 Sherman Way, Canoga Park, Calif.

BUD MEYER
Of Eddie Meyer Engineering, Hollywood.

DR. HERMAN CORN

FRED and NETTIE BERK

PHIL BLAZER
Of KVFM, KMET, Los Angeles, empire builder.

MR. and MRS. MORRIS BERENBAUM, JAX CARROLL, TOM DAGENAIS, BOB EUBANKS,
MELISSA GREENE, BRYAN JOSEPH, EDWARD L. LAMBERT, DR. MICHAEL MEYER of Cal
State Northridge.

PAUL KEYES

SID, HARRIET and MIKE MARWIL
Of Palm Springs.

TATSUJI NAGASHIMA
Of Tokyo, Japan, oddly enough.

DAVE ZENTNER, ANDY ETTINGER, MARETTA GAY, BIANCA McCAUSLAND and ELISE
MEYER
Of Pinnacle Books.

DR. M. LAWRENCE RUBINOFF and his magic stethoscope.

MR. and MRS. HENRY HALPERN, LOU and PHOEBE FEIN, and BILL GURALNICK of
Post 752, Jewish War Veterans.

LARRY and ANN KRUSS, HARVEY and ANNE LEVINE, KEN and BEVERLY LEVINE,
RICHARD and MARCIA MEDNICK, RALPH, RUTH MEHLWORM, DR GERALD and JOY
PICUS, MIKE and JEAN ROZENBLUM, DR. KEN and MARTI SCHWARTZ, LEN and FRAN
ROSENFIELD, MIKE PERLMUTTER GIL and FRAN SMUGAR, DR JACK and NINA LEE.

SAUL ROSSIEN

(COMMERCIAL BREAK NUMBER EIGHT: Let us review. We buy "The Oddfather" and
"Jonathan Segal Chicken," eat at the Tempura Inn, catch the acts of Mark
Russell and Paul Gray, try the garlic bread at Anna's and are so Inspired
by all of this that we naturally contribute to the Israeli Emergency
Fund. The train of cool logic can not be derailed.)

AL, FRAN and KAREN GORI

THE RISING BELL
Newspaper of the Hebrew Orphans Association of N.Y.C.

SHELLY WAX, CARL IRI and MARILYN ALVARADO
Of Playboy.

STEVE KUNES
Of WNHS, Neshaminy High School, Langhome, Pa.

VICTORIA JAMES and CONNIE CAMERON
Of KPLM-TV, Palm Springs.

SARA GOERKE
Of the Woodland Hills, Calif., Library.

MRS. ALPHA HAMMOND
Of the Red Cross, Naval Hospital, San Diego.

ROGER STERLING
Of The Las Virgenes Enterprise, Calabasas, Calif.

BUD JOHNS
Of Levi Strauss & Co., San Francisco.

JUSTIN CLOUSER
Of the Walden Book Store, Matoon, Illinois.

TERRY and DONNA BALLARD

IRA COOK
Of American Forces Radio.

LEN and ESTHER ROSS, INA GOLDFIELD and SID and BUNNY SHORE of The Shore
Club, Hulmeville, Bucks County, Pa.

And, of course,
WILBUR and NANCY LEVINE
Of Poughkeepsie, N.Y.

ONE

Now the sun had begun to drop behind the Black Hills of South Dakota. With the encroachment of darkness the thousands of vacationers who had gazed at Mount Rushmore to venerate the great stone faces of Washington, Jefferson, Lincoln and Teddy Roosevelt were meandering down the trails to their campsites. Imbued with a renewed sense of old-fashioned patriotism they had left their hearts and minds with the stone sentinels peering over the valley. And typical Americans that they were they had also left mounds of Budweiser cans, greasy Chicken Delight buckets, half-nibbled Hostess Twinkies and, in one extreme case, three rotten, whining kids who had been given a Union 76 road map, a day's supply of beef jerky and told to fend for themselves. ("Bunky, Cindy, Barry, it's not that mommy and daddy don't love you. It's just that, well, we don't ever want to see you again.")

Anyone standing on the hilltop would have been awestruck at what the immortal Wordsworth would have called "a host of golden daffodils," until closer examination would have revealed these posies as a stream of discarded yellow Kodak film boxes.

With the obligatory visitation to the shrine duly checked off, these hardy descendants of the pioneers would return to their campers and motels to get down to the real purpose of their pilgrimage: an all-night round of partying during which the Seagram & Seven would flow like mother's milk and at least one individual liberated by the uninhibiting sauce would try to make an unnatural maneuver toward an elk.

As the purple mantle of night spread over the landscape, the sun quit the West to make its appointed rounds in the East, illuminating masses headed for a Shinto shrine in Kyoto, the headshrinkers of Borneo hard at work making sure they had not mistakenly lopped off a Sanforized head, and wiry aborigines making equally strange maneuvers toward Koala bears at Alice Springs.

To the average Joe snapping away with his Polaroid, the great foursome seemed as majestic as ever. Only Gutzon Borglum, the genius who had designed and supervised the carving of this Presidential pantheon, would have noticed something amiss with the visages... lines of stress around Washington's brow,

Lincoln's beard losing its well-brushed look, darkening circles around Jefferson's eyes and a tightening of the lips of Teddy Roosevelt, which either led one to believe he was stifling an urge to yell "charge!" or suppressing a vicious gas pain. Borglum would have attributed these facial mutations to perfectly understandable natural causes, the debilitating effects of wind and water erosion. But the mighty granite faces knew better as they spoke to each other on the night wind.

Washington, eldest of the statesmen, was the first to break the silence. "Gentlemen, I have not endured such strain since Valley Forge. As bad as it was there, at least once a week we could sneak into Trenton and pick up a pint of Dolly Madison's Ice Cream."

"Yes," reminisced Jefferson. "My favorite was always vanilla and yours, George, was, of course, cherry, in order to keep that cockamamie legend going. Well, at least that cherry tree story was not as harmful as that other shtick you had going, throwing silver dollars across the river."

"What was so bad about the silver dollar?" Washington said with some testiness.

"It established a ridiculous precedent... throwing money across the water... which we today call foreign aid."

"Oh, yeah," Washington bristled. "Anything you ever wrote that was half-decent you stole. I heard about you keeping Tom Paine in the closet, doing your rewrites and paying him scale."

"Bully!" cried Teddy Roosevelt, "Bully!"

"And I can do without that constant 'Bully! Bully! Bully!' " Washington snarled. "To me the whole thing is bully shit! Why don't you go back up San Juan Hill and get a case of Roughrider Rash?"

"Gentlemen," said Lincoln, ever the peacemaker. "Why do we immortals bicker amongst one another? Why are we so irritable and haggard?"

"Because we can't sleep, that's why," said Washington. "Night after night something behind me on the cliff is causing that horrible clangor and pounding. Abe, you're the only one of us in position to see. What's going on up here?"

"It's a man, a man who comes to this place every night who's doing something strange. Every once in awhile I see his maddened beady eyes reflected in the moonlight." Lincoln glanced at the top of the granite bluff. "Jumpin' Jehosophat, here he comes again!"

Up the trail, those aforementioned beady eyes and all that went with them bobbed on the back of a malodorous pack mule, loaded down with the tools of his mysterious nightly trade. The intruder dismounted, flung a rope over the cliff and began to shinny down with one hand, his other clutching a five-pound sledgehammer. Soon he was swinging the sledge and with each blow an echo reverberated throughout the valley, causing the faces to wince at the prospect of another long, sleepless night. Insane cackling accompanied each bite of the hammer.

"He's mad," Jefferson whispered to his shocked mountain mates. "Listen how he talks to himself with no letup."

"No surprise," said a weary Washington. "Talking is his way of life. The mighty Mississippi would be proud to own a mouth like that."

As though he had heard the general's contemptuous aside, the intruder stiffened in anger. "Revile me as you wish. In a few days you will learn of my magnificence. I shall tower above you all. Soon, soon, soon!" and he renewed his frenzied pounding, confident of the ultimate success of a plan which even at that moment was in motion.

TWO

To the popping of photographers' flashbulbs the president of the United States with a grand flourish scrawled his signature on the parchment, his vice president beaming in approval, and so suffused with the excitement of the moment that he quaffed a glass of ouzo, made a little joke about his Mediterranean heritage ("I guess I'm in the Greek Social Register now—or as we call it *ouzo!*"), and broke into a spirited Zorba-like dance, kicking several Democratic congressmen who had come to witness the signing in the Oval Room.

"Well, it's a law now," the president smiled, lifting from a breast pocket his battery-powered Norelco and the shaver's triangular face, those two wide eyes and round mouth, said to its component parts underneath: *Here we go again.* The chief executive ran it around his black jowls in several quick maneuvers, leaving the kind of swirling paths usually associated with contour plowing in Nebraska. "According to the terms of this bill no male politician from the Northeast who has an estate in Hyannisport and pronounces Cuba 'Cuber' will be eligible to run for the Presidency in 1976."

There was a buzzing from the intimate group 14
of reporters who had been allowed into his office for a few brief questions.

"Mr. President. I'm Creston, *New York Times.* Can we discern a pattern in this bill and several others like it enacted in the past few weeks, bills, for instance, which make ineligible for presidential consideration anyone whose name rhymes with "dusky," or anyone who has the same name as the Democratic candidate in 1952 and 1956, or anyone who is tall and handsome and has been mayor of New York City? The way things are now, the only ticket the Democrats can field in 1976 is one made up of Lester Maddox and Jane Fonda, hardly a showstopper."

The president left that unanswered, but looked at the questioner with curiosity. What was this journalist doing here, and how had he survived the recent presidentially-ordered B-52 air strike on the *New York Times* building? The bill now a matter of law, the chief executive began the time-honored ritual of distributing the ceremonial pens to the onlookers: gleaming twenty-four-carat-gold Mark Cross pens to the GOP representatives, and twenty-nine cent Bic Bananas (which were bugged) to the Democrats.

Then he signed Bill 927, extending the benefits of the oil depletion allowance provision by permitting corporate leaders to achieve substantial tax breaks on their Ronson lighters. He pursed his mouth into a grimace for he could feel that unstoppable black beard forcing its way through the pores of his face and he again felt compelled to pick up the Norelco and zip it away. Darn it, he thought, that poet was dead wrong. *I am the forest primeval.*

"Daddy! Daddy!" The president spun at the familiar sound of his lovely, dark-haired younger daughter's trill. She came loping across the carpet crying, "I've only got one cavity!"

"Great!" her father said, allowing a rare smile to brighten that taciturn face. "How did you do it, honey?"

"Crest," his daughter replied with a delighted giggle.

"Yes," intoned the president's favorite religious leader, who stood by in his Brooks Brothers suit. "Crest. Even *He* would have used it."

Planting a kiss on her daddy's cheek and whispering "shave," she bounced out of the office and into the Rose Garden where a small crowd awaited her for the signing of the proclamation for Peanut Butter and Jelly Week.

"Mr. President?"

"Ah, yes, Mrs. McClintock of the Affiliated Pennysavers Shopping Center throwaway newspaper chain. What's your question, Hattie?"

"Sir," she said, her hooked needle at the ready, prepared to crochet his answer into a bedspread she was working on, "how are you tackling this school desegregation issue?"

"We gave that a lot of thought," he said, running the Norelco under his jowls. "We know busing is a touchy business, so we've decided to abolish it. No buses, but what we plan to do is to put the schools themselves on wheels so that they can cruise all neighborhoods, both black and white, from nine to three, giving each mommy a chance to see her Johnny or Janie at least four times a day. Good solution, don't you think?" He lit up a rolled-up copy of the latest Gallup Poll showing his policies trailing by 75 percent—25 percent (in his own family), inhaled it, blew out three large smoke rings which connected in midair and became the Ballantine beer symbol (a neat trick, he thought; someday he'd have to do it in Staten Island and nail down the beer vote for the party), and awaited the next query.

"Sir, Reynolds of *Sierra Magazine*. What is the outcome of the Rand Corporation study of pollution?"

"Mr. Reynolds, I'm glad you asked me that. It's so easy to put the blame on the major corporations as the prime polluters in this country, because they are, but I was never one to take the easy way out. I believe all Americans should be involved in this fight, so I'm giving a contract to the Gladwynne Corporation, a major polluter, incidentally, which will supply every man, woman and child with a burlap bag and a long stick with a nail on the end of it and they'll police the whole country. This expenditure will be authorized in Bill 1990, my so-called A & E bill."

And all those who had been in the military grinned, remembering that A & E stood for "asses and elbows."

"My own personal fight against the desecration of our land," he stated solemnly, honing his face again with the Norelco, "is symbolized by this." He pointed to a five-foot mound of black facial nubs, a half-day's shaving, pressed an intercom button and an aide bounded in, shoved the black nubs into a laundry bag and disappeared. "My excess shaving hair will be utilized to fill up those horrible gouges in the earth left by strip-mining. If all those hairy kids, and Lord knows, I've got nothing against long hair..."

"*He* wore it," whispered his spiritual leader.

"Yes," the president went on, "if all the kids would cut their hair and similarly fill up those holes, Appalachia would be reborn again."

There was a ponderous clomping of jackboots and he turned to wave farewell to his former aides, Gerlichmann und Haldermann und Kleindienstmann, who were doing their final lockstep in the White House. Good lads, but their Watergate-related activities had forced a decision of dismissal. When they'd found their own names on his now-famous list of enemies, they'd gotten the message. He'd miss their zeal and devotion, but certainly not their constant singing of "Deutschland Uber Alles," which had unnerved those press people who had covered Berlin in the 1930s.

Petersen of the *Chicago Trib* caught the chief executive's eye. "Sir, there's been quite a storm about your latest Supreme Court nomination. Does this Alabama county courthouse bailiff really have the intellectual tools to don a black robe and become one of the Nine Old Men?"

Even through the rapidly growing beard could be seen a blush. "Uh, Mr. Petersen, there may be a slight period of mental readjustment necessary for Bailiff Bobby Roy Jenkins, for, as you might know from your researches, he's been far more at ease all these years in a white robe. But I think we do need that conservative Southerner on the Court for balance against all the conservative Northerners I've appointed. Mr. Jenkins will battle the forces of permissiveness staining our land. Any man who believes meter maids should bear sidearms and be licensed to at least wound overtime parkers is on the right path, I think."

As the conference wore on it was interrupted briefly for a photo with the president and Miss Teenage Orthodontia (which shrewdly locked in the overbite vote), the announcement of the all-time, all-star Roller Derby team which the president and his son-in-law had selected (nailing down the blue-collar taproom constituency), and then the grizzled United Press International correspondent stood up to ask the long-expected key question.

"Sir, in a few days, you, the vice president and your special advisor, Dr. Henry Kissingherr, will be emplaning to Vienna for the Parley to Effectuate Permanent Peace by Ending Revolutions we've all been hearing about. Can you explain its significance to us and the world?"

The president shaved and then quickly blew the black nubs off his pile of notes. "As you know, Mr. Allwet, we've been involved in the Strategic Arms Limitation Talks, or SALT, as we know them, for some time. Well, it's time we passed the SALT," he chuckled at his bon mot, "and got to PEPPER."

The press boys gave an answering chuckle; except Creston who sneezed. The mere mention of PEPPER was sufficient to set off his allergies. But Creston rallied and said, "Why are we seemingly bypassing the United Nations by staging big power talks?"

The Norelco zipped on. "Mr. Creston, I have always supported the UN but sad to say it has become an ineffectual tool for achieving global stability. True, it's a swell place for delegates to practice their high school French and it's given Danny Kaye a wonderful out of town locale to raise money for UNICEF and break in his new act. But generally its prime function has been the acceptance of an ever-increasing number of mini-states, the latest, my National Security Council tells me, a large wooden raft in the South Pacific manned by only five tipsy Portugese sailors who are already claiming UN membership, having a national anthem written by Burt Bacharach and a flag designed by Simplicity Patterns.

"I have come to the regretful conclusion that the UN can not bring the generation of peace I have promised. What will supply it is PEPPER, conceived by Dr. Kissingherr. He is a great believer in the kind of diplomacy practiced in the early nineteenth century at the Congress of Vienna where such immortal statesmen as Metternich, Von Humboldt, Castlereagh and the others met from 1814—15 to rebuild the Europe shattered by the Napoleonic Wars. Congress of Vienna Two will feature the major powers in a re-creation of that period with the aim of bringing world order by the intelligent balance of power."

"What are some of Dr. Kissingherr's PEPPER talk ideas?" said Slaboda of *The Trentonian*.

The president put another battery in the back of the Norelco, carved out a very acceptable figure-eight on his cheek that Peggy Fleming would have applauded, and said, "Under the doctor's plan the world would be divided into spheres of influence and within each sphere there will be allowed a certain amount of internal tension in order to let the various political forces work off steam, without jeopardizing the grand design. For instance, in one sphere there would be allotted funds for either one local revolution per decade or one soccer stadium, not both. Guerrilla movements would be permitted to assassinate two oppressive left- or right-wing dictators a year or get ten free dance lessons, not both. Deposed monarchs may either steal from their national treasuries a reasonable set amount each month or accept a lump sum payment, but not both."

"We can easily understand how these measures will relieve those sporadic uprisings, but, sir," asked DeWolf of the *Philadelphia Bulletin*, "what are the major U.S. bargaining positions? What are we willing to give for this world stability?"

"That would be tipping our cards," said the president. "Many a government would like to know that to readjust its own position, but we won't reveal that until Congress of Vienna Two."

The senior press member could see the president's fatigue by the way he was shaving—he had missed his face and had raked a swath across the lapel of his mohair suit (strangely, the mohair, which had taken on the characteristics of its owner, was growing back!) —and said, "Thank you, Mr. President," and the news conference was over.

But before these giants of the Fourth Estate could leave, the chief executive decided to end on an upbeat note. He snapped his fingers and from a closet vaulted the "Johnny Mann Stand Up and Cheer" organization; they went through a fast, rousing medley of patriotic favorites, did a sprightly dance number on his desk, and wound up positioning their bodies into the letters: YOU'RE A GRAND OLD FLAG... YOU'RE A HIGH FLYING FLAG. No easy task for an aggregation of only a dozen members. A handsome young fellow in a blazer and white ducks was hurt severely trying to be the letter R all by himself.

"Well, Mr. President," the veep said. "Has everything been sufficiently solidified for our fleet flight by whirring whirlybird to your rustic retreat during which our ozone odyssey will take us over the dastardly domiciles of the effete elite snobs and nattering nabobs of gloom and doom?"

"If you mean are we ready for the helicopter trip to Camp David, the answer is yes. And try to tone down the alliterations."

"Oh, may I have a presidential pardon for my frequent frenetic uninhibited usages of aleatory alliterations which I patently perceive are giving you a hammering headache."

"I said—cool it."

"Will the good doctor be joining us at Camp David?"

"No, he's been looking a trifle peaked since his shuttling back and forth to Indochina to clean up the mess, so I gave him a few days off. I think he's out west somewhere, so it'll be just you and me cleaning up the last-minute details, reviewing our bargaining positions, working on our welcome speeches..."

"Gee," the veep cut in. "I've got a funny monologue that Bob Hope sent over. There's a joke about no starch in the shirts that'll put Chou En Lai on the floor."

"I'm the president. I'll do the funny stuff." Already they could hear the din of the choppers coming down in the Rose Garden and they quickened their pace toward the helipad.

"Good luck, Mr. President," smiled his personal secretary who, as soon as she saw her celebrated boss depart, took out of her typewriter a presidential letter to Pat Boone praising the crooner for personally pushing milk sales up by forty-five percent and reinserted Chapter IV of her secret diary, *I Was The President's Private Secretary,* (for which she had already received a $35,000 advance from Simone & Schusser). The president also was greeted fulsomely by a janitor who between moppings was at work on *I Was The President's Cleanupman* ($40,000 advance, Brandon House) ; the elevator man ($50,000 advance, Dabbleday, for *I Lifted The President To The Heights*) ; but got only a surly nod from a gardener who was deeply into *I Pruned The President's Pansies,* for which he had garnered no interest as yet but was writing sheerly on spec.

Waving a cheery farewell to the press, the president and the veep clambered aboard Chopper One, snuggled into their seats and Major General Blane Westcott, the officer who kept the deadly black box always within five feet of his commander in chief, took his customary back seat. As always he felt a chill from the weight of the box on his lap, for it was a literal Pandora's box of horror, and one code word from the president would activate a series of ciphers sending bomber wings and ICBMs and Polaris subs into a twentieth century Armageddon.

Happily, he felt no pressure at the moment for this month's code word was "Amnesty," one the president was unlikely to use in normal conversation. But last month's war-starting word, "hello," had seemed to be a real booboo on the part of the Pentagon, for the president had had to exercise enormous mental control to avoid saying it, beginning his telephonic conversations and shaking hands with Congressional leaders with the words "so long," and at a soiree requesting the band to play "Goodbye, Dolly."

The huge blades spun like a beanie gone mad and the craft quickly lifted to its 3,000-foot cruising range. Up with it rose the backup chopper, crammed with Secret Servicemen. They would fly within 500 feet of the president during the brief journey to the mountains.

Below him spread the vastness of the capital, and he made a mental note to have something done about changing the appearance of the 505-foot Washington monument. It would not be fitting in his violently antidrug administration to have a national symbol that looked like a gigantic hypodermic needle. Now Chopper One was over the luxurious verdure of Maryland, with its neat rows of development housing, the haze from garbage dumps and factories, ribbons of highways jammed with bumper-to-bumper traffic, eight-dollar motels, nineteen-cent hamburger joints, and a billboard snarling its defiant message:

AMERICA, LOVE IT OR LEAVE IT, and he looked down upon all that he had made and saw that it was good.

The pilot's voice pierced his reverie. "Sir, there's something kind of unusual. If you glance out our starboard side you can get a fine view of the Goodtire blimp."

"Golly," the president said with boyish gusto. "I've always wanted a ride in one of those babies.

Why don't you move in a little closer for a better look?" He nudged his veep in the ribs. "There it is, free enterprise on the hoof. Say, look, there's an electronic ribbon of lights giving all the latest sports news. Son of a gun, Aaron hit another one!"

"Sir," and the pilot's voice held a shade of anxiety, "it's getting too close to our flight path. I'd better warn them off."

"Oh wait," said the president. "What's that bulletin? 'Yankees trade two pitchers' wives to Red Sox for a shortstop and a utility hooker...' " But now the pilot seemed totally unnerved. He and his backup pilot snapped angry messages: "Goodtire blimp, you're too close... too damn close..." And their voices were now shrill and quivering.

But the great silver cigar bore down.

"Jesus, we can't get out of the way," the Chopper One pilot yelled. There was a flash of something glinting in the twilight, a whooshing noise and a great harpoon snaked out of the blimp's gondola, entwining itself around the rotary. The president and veep were buffeted suddenly, the former's Norelco fell from his hand, the horrified pilot screamed one final "Mayday!" to the backup, but then his voice was drowned by the clatter of the spinning Chopper One.

An iron voice on a loudspeaker said coolly, "Chopper Two, desist from your activities. The president and vice president are prisoners. Any foolish bravado will needlessly endanger their lives. Fly off and do not attempt to follow. We have scanning devices. Maintain strict radio silence. You will be contacted at a time of our choosing."

And as dramatically as it had come, the blimp loped away into a cloud bank, the helpless captive Chopper One being reeled in toward the gondola by the incredible device which had pinioned it like the rapid-fire tongue of a frog lashing out at a fly.

Sitting helplessly at the controls, the backup pilot was smitten by a horrible thought: within the very shadow of the

Capitol, the president and vice president of the United States were prisoners of some unknown force in the very land of the free that they had been elected to govern.

THREE

Standing in front of the full-length mirror, the secretary of state gave himself the once-over. The white bow tie was adjusted, a flick of a hanky sent a dust particle spinning off his patent leather shoes and he gave his silvery tresses a final jet of Command hair spray. Not bad, he thought admiringly, considering the elegant figure in the formal outfit who smiled back at him with supreme confidence. As was his wont when he donned formal clothes he found himself suddenly possessed of a need to do a Fred Astaire dance step, finishing with a high kick that sent the globe of the world on his desk bouncing into a wastebasket.

Screw you, world! Tonight I'm going on the town.

Holding a phantom Ginger Rogers in his arms and crooning, "I'm puttin' on my top hat... puttin' on my white tie... fixin' up my tails," he went through a series of dazzling dips and breaks which found him bounding over couches and chairs, ultimately ending up in an intimate position with the hat rack in the corner.

Contrasted with the other pressing engagements he'd had, tonight's diplomatic dinner at the Republic of Umgowah embassy would be a welcome respite. This tiny Congo Basin nation, whose principal export was chimpanzees for Tarzan pictures and certain bizarre strains of tropical disease, usually put on a magnificent spread. Their cream of hyena soup was a prime favorite in Washington circles, the hippo loaf a real stick-to-the-ribs main dish, and the cobra sherbet a delight that Baskin-Robbins was dying to make flavor # 32.

Then came the phone call and the two terse words that snapped him out of his filmic fantasy: "Product 19."

With frightening speed the last black hair on his sideburns turned snowy white, the carnation in his lapel wilted into a soggy mass and, legs atremble, he wobbled to the safe behind the portrait of the president. Four quick spins popped it open and he was holding a white envelope with the legend "Product 19" on its face. He ripped it open and read:

"In the event the president and vice president are imprisoned, incapacitated, or otherwise unavailable, the following plan will go into effect. Step one..."

As he read it, his fingers were already untying his tie and he moved to the closet in the rear.

In the Pentagon, the head of the Joint Chiefs of Staff, his head bent over in the glow of a small desk lamp, was looking at the plans for the projected *Phallus* anti-anti-anti-ballistic missile which would intercept any incoming Soviet missile and neutralize it by doing lewd things to it. It had come down to a choice between *Phallus* and *Fleet,* another ABM system, the latter a gigantic enema which also would intercept hostile rockets and clean them out thoroughly. Racked suddenly by a childhood memory, his mother's cooing voice saying, "Just another little more water, darling," he tightened his sphincter, gnashed his teeth in distaste. Then and there he opted for *Phallus,* stamped his O.K. on the plans, and threw the *Fleet* proposal into the john and flushed it down with his memories.

Then came the phone call, the two words that sent a convulsion through him and caused his oak-leaf cluster to wither, turn brown and die, and he was on his way to his office closet.

Similar scenes occurred in the head offices of the CIA, the FBI, and the other branches that comprised the intelligence community... quick phone calls and distinguished men furtively diving into their closets.

"And so, ladies and gentlemen," the First Lady concluded to the front portico audience, a brave smile on her face masking the horrible anxiety in her heart that had come with the shocking report from Camp David, "as we choose Miss Middle America, we choose a lovely lady so reflective of rural values, the homespun stock that made our country what it is today."

She placed the garland of alfalfa and beet root upon the braided blonde head of the winner, a rather bulky female in a somewhat unstylish but quite serviceable dress made of a checkered Ralston Purina feed sack. The audience applauded politely, but a *Women's Wear Daily* reporter said to a colleague from *Vogue,* "My God, where did they get those broads... from the taxi squad of the Green Bay Packers?"

"Look at the legs of the winner. I've never seen tree trunks in pantyhose before. I know farm women work hard but this one could take out a threshing machine with one punch," the *Vogue* columnist snickered.

"And the other contestants. Have you ever seen such beef in your life? Those Ann Sheridan hairdos, those Joan Crawford shoulders? And look at Miss Congeniality over there. Have you ever seen combat boots with ankle straps? Incidentally, it's a funny thing—this contest wasn't even on the first lady's social schedule for today."

"I understand it was a last-minute insertion, probably a bid for the farm vote."

"And now," the First Lady was saying, "these lovely contestants and I will dine together as is customary. We girls have an awful lot to talk about." With a wave she led the two dozen muscular ladies into the White House and the door slammed shut.

In a secret conference room the charade ended: the hastily improvised Miss Middle America beauty pageant which was in actuality step one of the Product 19 operation.

With a sigh of relief the secretary of state unhinged his blond wig, wiped off his Max Factor pancake makeup and noticed that the Joint Chiefs of Staff were now slipping out of their girdles with similar sighs of relief. Playtex had done its part for America.

The CIA chief put a consoling arm around the First Lady. "My dear, thanks so much for letting us pull you away from the National Gallery of Art, where you were officiating at the installation of the King family portraits. It was most important that this bogus beauty contest be staged to admit us all into the White House. If the press boys had seen dozens of black limos pulling up they would have smelled something funny."

Even as he said this his nostrils did, indeed, smell something funny, a whiff of Chanel Number 19 on the wrist of the Chief of Naval Intelligence which was producing an odd effect on the chief of Army Intelligence.

The First Lady gone from the room, the heads of government sat, their faces grim.

"Gentlemen," spoke the CIA boss. "We have a crisis of unparalleled proportions. Under our very noses the president and vice president of the United States have been kidnapped under circumstance we are familiar with now, if you will all glance at your 'Eyes Only' memorandum."

"In the interest of time I suggest we call in the backup chopper pilot," FBI said, typically to the point.

In moments Marine Captain Wayne Trescott, a typically sinewy jarhead, stood before the council of war. Unfolding his narrative in laconic style, he emphasized highlights of the story by chopping his karate-callused hand down savagely, splintering large sections of the conference table which the naval chieftain began to glue together. In a few moments he had a fair replica of *Old Ironsides* in front of him.

"We've checked with the Goodtire people," the FBI noted. "The blimp was originally rented in Miami two days ago by a representative of a Hollywood film production company. He claimed he was going to use it for *The Totie Fields Story* and that the blimp was supposed to play the part of Totie as a child. Seemed perfectly logical, and they paid good money for it."

"And it's also logical," said the secretary of state, "that someone doesn't want our president and his running mate to attend the PEPPER talks six days hence. Some dissident element in China or Russia?"

"Maybe that's what they want us to think," said Navy.

"Maybe they want us to chase all over the globe while all the time it's merely a case of a simple, everyday presidential kidnapping," Army Intelligence puffed on his pipe.

"If it is," said CIA, "we'll be getting the ransom terms any minute now... they could ask for anything... fifty, one hundred, two hundred million dollars. And we'll have to give it to 'em. It's the president of the United States at stake. Only one thing bothers me. What if they want cash?"

"Cash? That's trouble," said FBI. "Maybe they'll take Mississippi as a down payment?"

"If you were a kidnapper, would *you* take Mississippi as a down payment?" asked CIA.

"Good point," FBI said. "I would say go as high as Rhode Island and then stop; maybe we can settle for Kansas."

"Well, it can't be more than two hundred million," said Treasury, consulting some documents. "According to the Wage-Price Freeze Phase Eight no kidnapper can make more than 200 million. I have the figures right here... skyjacking of a B-52 jet fifty million dollars, theft of nuclear weapon seventy-five million, theft of Andromeda strain baccilli one hundred million dollars..."

"Gentlemen, we're going nowhere. The PEPPER talks are the most significant development in modern history. He's got to be there. If he doesn't show, the other major powers will think God knows what. That maybe America has been seized by a coup— that it's politically unreliable—that maybe they'd better strike against us before we do something insane against them." CIA pounded the table. "We've got to figure out who's behind this plot and marshall our best minds against it!"

There was silence at the table, broken only by the sound of the three-inch portable Sony television in the pocket of the FBI director. When they glowered at him, he said apologetically, "Aw, guys, it's Sunday night. You don't expect me to miss 'Columbo,' do you?"

"Our best mind isn't even here," CIA said with a bitter smile. "If there's one man in the world with sufficient gray matter to get to the bottom of this it's..."

"Oh, no," said the secretary of state, biting his lip in childish petulance. "Not him. He gets all the glory assignments... the trips to Paris, China, Russia. He gets his damn face on the cover of *Time* and *Newsweek,* and, I—the head of the State Department— the best I get is a trip to El Salvador to represent Old Glory at the opening of the trichinosis festival. And he's diminished the prestige of State Department so drastically that even when I am allowed out of the country I have to put on my son's denim jacket, carry a guitar and go on student standby."

"You're forgetting one thing, gentlemen," said CIA. "At this very moment the chief may be undergoing diabolical torture. He could be revealing secret base locations, nuclear weapons development, treaties, perhaps even the source of his campaign contributions."

"Oh, my God, not that!" whimpered the attorney general.

"There isn't one man in this room who hasn't been dwarfed by our dear Herr Doktor's brilliance, but this is no time for grudges." A round of "Here, here" swept around the table as CIA picked up a gold phone. "Operator, get me Beverly Hills, California... Crestview 5-7541."

FOUR

In the ultra-posh "A" section of Beverly Hills —which by municipal ordinance starts at the Beverly Hills Hotel, wends its way north of Sunset Boulevard, and winds up in a numbered Swiss bank account—the usual late afternoon activities were being carried on under a warm, ninety-degree sun. The remnants of many party platters in various backyards, catered by Nate 'N Al's, were beginning to atrophy in the heat, and now the scent of sunburnt lox and curdling Dannon Yogurt was pervasive, and on some patios the eyes of the nibbled whitefish seemed to say: "Why me? There I was, minding my own business, swimming along, and the next thing I knew there I am propped up against some onions. Yes, I can attest to the Sturgeon-General's Report. As far as a fish is concerned, smoking can be hazardous to your health."

Throughout the somnolent afternoon resounded the puck-puck of tennis racket against ball on a hundred private clay courts. In the cabanas could be heard a sound very similar to the puck-puck, this coming from starlets eager to show producers why they should be cast in their forthcoming motion pictures.

Of all the opulent mansions in the area—their driveways strewn with Rolls Royces, Mercedes 600s, and the even more revered reconditioned 1931 Ford Model-A classic antique coupes—none was more so than the one reached by gunning your vehicle down Benedict Canyon to Franklin Pangbom Drive, making a sharp left at Barton MacLane Road, and thence to the top of Jack Norton Way, which like its drunken namesake weaved its way over the hills. At 1919 Norton Way stood the palatial home of movie queen Jill St. James, upon whose gate was the family motto: *"Ad astra per alimonia."*

Outside stood a car which did not seem to belong in the plush ambience, a ratty Volkswagen with a faded bumpersticker: FOUR MORE YEARS.

"It is to Jill St. James's mansion," Joyce Jabber, leading Hollywood gossip columnist, had written, "that the pear-shaped, double-chinned, bespectacled, yet thoroughly fascinating, superdiplomat most often comes. True, he has dated in the past such film lovelies as Sally Ballerman, Raquel Squelch, and publicity-conscious Judy Blue, but this gutsy, leggy, auburntressed charmer seems to have the key to the attache case of his heart. Who knows what the attraction is? Her forty-five-room mansion? Her 160 I.Q.? Or her 38-24-36? Whatever it is, Miss St. James has got Henry's number."

The aforementioned domicile was a typical illustration of Hollywood architecture, part Spanish, part Tudor, part French Normandy and the balance done up in modern Safeway Supermarket.

Sprawling over a ten-acre plot, ringed by a high stucco wall, was a layout that included six swimming pools, each shaped in the replica of one of her ex-husbands... crooners, playboys, socialites, etc... In the far end of the Bernie Braverman pool— this one filled with seltzer in honor of her last spouse, a Seventh Avenue dress tycoon—splashed a bulky man who shook off millions of tiny carbonated bubbles and squinted through his water-smeared horn-rimmed glasses.

"Henry," laughed the beauty lying on a chaise, applying Vitamin B cream to her C-cups, Vitamin C to her spectacularly turned legs and Vitamin E where it would do the most good. "I'm sure that black suit and regimental tie is *de rigueur* for summit conferences, but why do you have to wear them in a swimming pool?"

With as much dignity as a man surrounded by seltzer can muster, the individual pulled himself out of the pool, walked to the film goddess's side and clicked his heels. "It is quite necessary, my dear. You must understand that a man in my position is constantly at his president's beck and call. This way I can be ready at a moment's notice. As you can see, this suit is a drip-dry." Even as he spoke, the sound of fabric repelling water was quite audible.

Shaking out the last drops of seltzer, Dr. Henry A. Kissingherr, the special advisor to the president of the United States, moved to the splayed out Miss St. James and put his arms around her creamy shoulders. Even through the thick lenses she could see the owlish eyes beseeching her for *l'amour.*

Kittenishly she pushed him away. "Oh, no, Henry."

"So?" he said in his soft Bavarian accent. "I have offended you?"

"Oh, Henry. Why make a move like some Malibu Beach stud? Those kind of men are a dime a dozen. I can get that brute force crap any time I want it, but I've grown up since my *Bikini Beach* movie days. The key to me is your mind, Henry, that fabulous mind. That's what turns me on."

"Ach," he sighed, again deeply perturbed that he was to be denied the pleasures of any ordinary man, a conquest preceded by nothing more intellectual than a good substantial smash in the mouth. How he envied those men in wraparound sunglasses, lithe blond men of broad shoulders and narrow hips who exuded the lean hardness of Western stars. No, it was not his body women wanted so much as the aura of power that swirled around his professorial head, the hints of great matters of state, of clandestine meetings, of earth-shattering decisions. Alas, he knew all this and again would play the game.

"Tell me, Henry, tell me what I want to hear..." She leaned back and took a deep drag on a Virginia Slim cigarette, the special brand for women. You've come a long way, baby, Dr. Kissingherr thought. You've even got your own special kind of emphysema.

Adjusting his glasses he looked at her with the detachment of a political science mentor. "The emergence of a third force in geopolitical affairs stemmed from the failure of the major nationstates to comprehend the reservoir of unfulfilled expectations."

"Oh, unfulfilled expectations! Say it again..."

"Naturally where there is a power vacuum it will be filled by internal forces, those which reflect the hopes and ambitions of the smaller powers recently liberated from the yoke of colonialism."

Her lips had begun to part. "Oh, God, the yoke of colonialism! Go on, Henry..."

"Hence the political realities dictated the coalescence of the hitherto unaligned nations and so in the historic conference at Bandung..."

"Oh, Bandung... say Bandung again. When you say it it sounds like a sonnet from Elizabeth Barrett Browning."

"Ban—dung," He let the name roll over his lips into two distinct syllables and noticed she had begun a sort of thrashing about on her chaise lounge.

"Ban—dung," he repeated, and wondered why she was being aroused by two syllables which when taken out of their Indonesian context and transliterated into English meant "stop shit."

"Oh, Henry," she murmured and now her breath was coming in short staccato bursts, a flush stole over her face, there was a sudden swelling of her Vesuvian breasts.

Knowing quite well he had her staggering on the ropes of the Ring of Love, vulnerable to a finishing combination, he fired his one-two punch. "Dealing with this Third World will involve the scrapping of ancient shibboleths regarding the underdeveloped nations," and a fast glance apprised him that although some of these nations were underdeveloped, Jill St. James was decidedly not.

"Oh, God... Scrapping of ancient shibboleths! Oh, Henry..."

"It will behoove the so-called advanced nations to treat as equal partners these emerging Third Worlders by establishing trade, lending aid, and financing capital equipment."

"What do you think of *my* capital equipment, Henry?" she breathed.

"Capital!" he responded. "Your breasts are like North and South Vietnam, separated by a demilitarized zone of indescribable loveliness."

With a Kissingherr kiss he crossed into that DMZ, knowing full well he was guilty of a territorial violation, and not giving a damn. She writhed and he felt butterfly kisses at his earlobes. "Your navel is the great fertile delta of the Nile," and eagerly he was flooding that delta with more strategically placed kisses hoping that if the passion continued he would pick up a piece of Aswan Dam. She shuddered and he tugged off her wispy mono-kini bottom, and, like the political party he was working for, he made a telling inroad into the Deep South.

"Oh, Henry, oh Henry!" she was shrieking. "Am I ready for love?"

"My *liebschen,* as we have often said about Southeast Asia, I definitely see a light at the end of the tunnel."

He stripped off his thoroughly dry drip-dry and proceeded to the physical climax for which the verbal foreplay had paved the way.

Now she was his to do with as he chose and he alternated sexual positions with detailed descriptions of the various positions of the contending parties at the Geneva Accords. A heated squeeze of breast, an equally heated explanation of the Treaty of Brest-Litovsk... sexual congress, an analysis of the Congress of Vienna... now, more congress, less Vienna... her entreaty and sigh, his Treaty of Versailles... Suddenly he was mumbling about the Reichstag Putsch and she was mumbling back, "Putsch your arms around me, honey, hold me tight." On it raged, this symbiosis of international diplomacy and Kraft-Ebbing and after a shattering climax between her Yalta and his Four Freedoms, his craft now really ebbing, she sobbed, snuggled against his bulbous middle and whispered in adoration, "Now I know why they call you Dr. Strangelove. Oh, Henry..."

The spell was shattered by the clattering of a helicopter swooping dangerously low over the estate, there was a black object hurtling out of the chopper door and a man in a wet suit hit the pool with a great splash, causing a geyser to spray over their heated bodies.

"A thousand pardons, Dr. Kissingherr," the man called out. "Product 19."

The doctor's mouth tightened, he slipped with celerity back into his drip-dry, muttered a hasty apology to the startled Miss St. James and began to climb the ladder leading to the hovering aircraft. Within seconds it was a disappearing dot in the Hollywood haze and Jill St. James shivered, for she knew her paramour was being summoned to God only knew what.

And she prayed fervently that, whatever it was, she would see her Sensuous Diplomat again.

FIVE

Operation Quaker Snatchback—the project to return the president to his rightful place—had been set up in a special room in the CIA headquarters at Langley, Virginia. Around a gigantic table sat the security chiefs of the government watching the flickering lights on a situation board run by a computer.

Thousands of agents had been pulled off their regular assignments surveilling subversives, malcontents, dissidents, which to this administration meant Democrats. They had already taken to the streets to check out the wispiest of clues. One agent had found a slip of paper under his windshield advising him to be at a certain location at 9 A.M., took it to be a secret communication and spent an entire morning at a carwash, waiting for a contact and watching his Mercury Montego after the ninth immersion in harsh detergents come out shrunken into a Toyota. When he noticed 5,000 other CIA operatives also putting their vehicles through the wash he realized all had been victimized by an overly aggressive handbill advertising campaign.

Dr. Kissingherr, already fatigued before his monumental task was to begin, was now in a black sedan motoring through the lush Virginia countryside. Ach, that Worldways Airlines flight from LAX had been insufferable. True, he realized the fierce competition for passengers now raging among the major carriers was necessary to attract clientele, but they had long gone past the stage of cute hostesses and gourmet meals. This particular flight had featured three distinct categories of motion pictures: *Dumbo* for the G-rated crowd, *The Last Dumbo in Paris* for the R-crowd, and Dumbo in *Deep Trunk* for the anything goes bunch. He had not minded the cocktail pianist in the lounge, but the entire production of *Cabaret,* including Joel Grey dancing and singing "Wilkummen" on the wing of the 747, proved an unnerving sight.

"Everything is in readiness for you, Dr. Kissingherr," said the CIA chief, the car bearing down on its destination. The doctor began to spot signs strewn along the way: THIS IS NOT THE ROAD TO THE C.I.A., and further on, WE SWEAR TO GO THE C.I.A. IS NOT

IN THIS AREA… and a third, IF YOU DO SEE A BUILDING MARKED "C.I.A."
IT ONLY STANDS FOR "CONGREGATION ISAAC ABRAHAM."

"We do our best to keep our base inconspicuous," the CIA
chief said proudly. "As a cover we even have Orthodox Jewish
services." Even as he spoke ten obviously Anglo-Saxon types
whipped on skullcaps and prayer shawls and began to chant
what was ostensibly meant to be an ancient Hebraic prayer, but
somehow it came out sounding like "Beer Barrel Polka."

Forgive them, Oh God of Israel; they know not what they do,
whispered the Jewish heart of Dr. Henry Kissingherr.

Inside the situation room he met a sea of bewildered faces,
eyes pleading silently: *Dr. Kissingherr, help America in its hour of
need.*

Except the blazing jealous eyes of the secretary of state,
whose disdain for this foreign-born usurper of power was
evident on his patrician face.

The CIA boss got to the point. "Gentlemen, for the sake
of brevity I suggest we skip the singing of 'The Star Spangled
Banner' and," he nodded toward the doctor, " 'Hatikvah.' Let us
bring Dr. Kissingherr up to date."

Army Intelligence stood up. "Gentlemen, here's a
communique: the blimp was found four hours ago in Topeka,
Kansas."

"Dammit! That thing has been on the ground for four hours
and nobody let us know?" snapped Navy Intelligence. "Why?"

"Well, it seems it was abandoned outside the local Weight
Watchers chapter. The ladies mistook it for a prospective
new member and were so embarrassed by its girth they were
ashamed to ask it any questions. They're a very sensitive bunch."

"Which means the president, the veep, the nuclear codecarrier and the pilot have long since been transferred to some
site on the ground. They could be anywhere in the U.S. by now,
or for that matter, on their way to a foreign country," FBI said
gloomily.

"My agents went over the blimp with a fine-tooth comb,"
reported the head of Secret Service. "There were no fingerprints."

"Then how do you know this was the blimp involved in the
kidnap?" said State.

"Simple. We," and the Secret Service dumped the contents
of an envelope onto the table, "found these scattered around the
gondola."

A thrill of horror sped through these hardened intelligence chiefs for lying there was a tell-tale trail of black facial nubs.

"That is an excellent sign," Dr. Kissingherr said sagaciously. "It means he is alive and shaving." Murmurs of approval echoed through the room. "Which signifies, gentlemen, that they do not intend him any physical harm, at least for the moment."

The secretary of state bit his lip savagely. *Why didn't I think of that?*

"And naturally, gents, there is no Hollywood producer currently involved in a Totie Fields film," said FBI, "so we drew a blank there. But the agent I sent around to the studios to check out the story hit paydirt. He's been signed for three guest shots with Efram Zimbalist Jr. on 'The FBI'."

"Gentlemen," Dr. Kissingherr's eyes swept the panel. "We may also assume that since the man who carries the black box has not been ordered to use it, that this unknown force does not plan to start a nuclear war either."

Again the doctor's cool logic cut like a knife into the festering carbuncle of jealousy in the heart of the secretary of state. *Dammit,* he thought, *why didn't I think of that?* And for the second time in his querulousness he bit his lip violently.

For the next hour the Operation Quaker Snatchback team kicked around all the possibilities in an intensive, headcracking session. Dossiers of all known political subversives were examined with meticulous detail. The board was flashing data fed to it by the computer concerning a group of arrests already made by hardhitting, fast-moving security teams. A wholesale coast-to-coast roundup of the Weathermen had been speedily accomplished by one CIA task force, but the agent in charge had been forced to admit they had hauled in the wrong bunch of Weathermen and in doing so denuded thousands of television stations of their forecasters, including Kelly Lange, crack Los Angeles meteorologist, snatched from her chart in mid-millibar.

Another grievous mistake had been made. Ordered to pull in the right-wing Minutemen, the FBI clerical staff had misspelled the name into Minutemaid and before it could be rectified an entire instant orange juice plant in Florida had been put behind bars. So it went throughout the night, men who normally operated with cool dispatch, were making understandable errors of judgement in this most dire of crises.

At three in the morning the doctor, still unflappable despite the strain that had put ugly red veins in the eyes of the other conferees and caused a run on Murine in every drugstore within a twenty-mile radius, stood up and said, "Gentlemen." A hush of respect fell over the table. When Henry Kissingherr spoke, his words were worth listening to. What would be the next pearl of wisdom to fall from his mouth?

"I suggest we send out for some coffee and Danish," he said.

All present murmured their agreement, except the envious secretary of state who glowered and thought, *Dammit! He scored again! Why didn't I think of that?* For a third time he sought to manifest his displeasure by biting his lip, but rolling his tongue around his already swollen mouth thought better of it and in frustration sank his teeth angrily into his assistant's lip. After all, what were flunkies for?

While the others munched away, the doctor scribbled some words on a yellow pad and at the conclusion of the snack stood up.

"I believe our first course of action is the dissemination of a cover story. The press will be told that the president and his party have sequestered themselves, are preparing for the PEPPER talks and will not be available for public statements."

"That's fine," said CIA, "but what if a crisis arises in some global hot spot and the press expects a comment. Then what?"

"Simple. Then we go to this." The doctor punched the play-button of a tape recorder. "This statement will go over national radio."

"My fellow Americans," came the calm, measured voice of the nation's leader. "In this hour of crisis you may rest assured that America's role will be examined in the light of all developments and our policy will proceed in accordance with our time-honored tradition of reason with firmness, of firmness with reason, of reasonably firm firmness and yet with a firmly reasonable reason."

"But that statement doesn't mean a damn thing!" exploded CIA in consternation.

"It got him elected," said the doctor, a winsome twinkle in his eye.

"That's okay for public consumption," said Navy Intelligence, "but suppose something big comes up that demands a face-to-face meeting with the Chief and, say, the Russian or Chinese ambassador?"

"We then go to Operation Duplication. Secretly on our payroll is nightclub comedian Danny Frye who does a spectacular physical and vocal impression of the president. If need be he will be coached by us and then stage the briefest of meetings with any top diplomat."

"You're going to let a comedian be president of the United States?" nastily interjected the secretary of state, inwardly gloating; at last he had found a chink in the kraut's armour.

"Gentlemen, this country has elected Grant, Harding, and Fillmore, to name just a few. The concept works."

So furious at being topped again by the Kissingherr wit was State that he kicked his assistant cruelly in the groin. "Fairchild, you're fired!" he told the startled young man.

"Well, we've got a few days to produce our leader in Vienna. If he doesn't show up at the PEPPER talks..." FBI gave a helpless shrug.

"I suggest," said Army Intelligence, "that because Dr. Kissingherr is so obviously on top of the situation that he be placed in charge of our unit and given as many men as he needs."

All the men I need, the Doctor thought, thousands of operatives covering every detail, but then he gave a secret smile, remembering an interview he had recently granted to Italian journalist Orafix Fallopiana. She had asked him, "Dr. Kissingherr, why do you play the lone hand?" He had answered, "Americans have always admired the solitary James Bond-John Wayne figure, the lone hero. This romantic, surprising character conforms to my nature because being alone has always been part of my style." And he knew that he had trapped himself into a decision.

"Gentlemen," the doctor raised his hand. "I am flattered, indeed, but may I make one small recommendation? I would prefer to be a lone operative in this business. If I am surrounded by legions of men, that will draw suspicion and publicity. I must work unencumbered."

Good, you bastard, thought the secretary of state. You swallowed your own press clippings. Go ahead and be the superhero and fall right on your hiney, Heinie.

"But, Doctor," Navy Intelligence said. "If you're going to be traipsing around the world alone you may be in personal physical danger. We've got to give you a crash course in weaponry and the martial arts."

"Ach, no," the doctor smiled ruefully. "As you can see by my unprepossessing physique I would not last ten seconds in a brawl with a Little League shortstop. And as for firearms, that is out of the question. Once I went hunting with the president of France in the Ardennes and it proved disastrous. He bagged two wild boars and the only thing I have to show for the escapade is the stuffed head of the Deputy Minister of Finance in my rec room. No, I shall use the only tool that a merciful God bestowed upon me." There was a strange catch of untypical humility in his accent. "My insuperable brain, the likes of which has not been seen on this earth."

Again came the murmurs of the approval, but by this time the bulky figure had gathered up his briefcase, clicked his heels and walked into the Virginia night, knowing not what would be his fate in the perilous days to come.

SIX

At 5:40 A.M. Chanticleer—the pet rooster of the Henry Thoreau Walden Pond Commune for Ecological Balance, Oneness of Nature, Cosmic Understanding, and Trading Stamp Redemption Center—climbed painfully onto a rail fence, shook his befuddled head, for someone in this fun-loving commune had slipped a little Mistala Wine into his chickenfeed, and crowed a note that shattered the morning silence.

Inside the geodesic dome which served as the main lodge for the inhabitants, those sons and daughters of the upper middle class who had fled its plastic technology to seek truth and beauty in a rough-hewn spartan atmosphere, stirred, then arose, turned off their electric blankets, cleaned their teeth with Water-Piks, started up their Silex coffeemakers, popped their homemade banana bread into Caloric ranges, worked out their stiffness of muscle in Jacuzzi whirlpool baths and made ready for another day of the pioneer life.

These refugees from big city civilization, who had dropped their old names of Tara, Robin Lynn, Shelly, Richie and Kevin, and now called each other Prudence, Zeb, Zeke, and Dan'l, slipped into their Levi's and buckskins and walked into the sunshine to survey the crops they had planted which would guarantee their survival in this South Dakota wilderness. The marijuana fields were doing splendidly, the peyote mushrooms almost fully grown, the opium poppies heavy with their sweetness. Yes, next Thanksgiving Day on the commune would truly be a high holiday, the turkey filled with the grooviest stuffing in creation.

Because they themselves had broken the bonds of their traditional upbringing they tended to treat with understanding and tolerance any others who were marching to the beat of a different drummer and in the past had hosted as communal guests the loincloth-clad Maharishi Heshi, the sinewy old mystic from India who had found his own salvation through prayer, fasting and $1,000-a-night lectures at colleges; Aquarius Applebaum, the new vogue in astrology, who had told them one night that Venus and Mars were leaving the ninth house of Jupiter to move into a condominium in Fort Lauderdale where the weather was nicer; and a string of rock philosophers, including the sensitive, alienated and lonely poet Rod McRuin, who dressed in Carol Channing's old clothes, had thrilled the young pioneers with his brand of soul-searching verse:

> "I once had a date with a girl named Myrtle,
> Who rode around town on a ten-ton turtle,
> So I dropped old Myrtle for a chick named Alice,
> Who in a fit of malice blew up Buckingham
>   Palace,
> So I gave her up for a lady named Lou,
> But when Lou served me stew-in-a-shoe I was
>   through,
> So I gave her up and I went back to Myrtle,
> But not to see her—I'm dating the turtle."

And so inured to the sight of oddball types were they, that they thought nothing of it when a man with a hood and his retinue had brought into the commune two individuals who were dead ringers for the president and vice president of the United States, plus two bound and gagged military men. "It's freaky, man, definitely an example of guerrilla theater!" enthused one of the communalists.

And thus in one of these lodges the kidnapped world leader, his veep, general and pilot sat tied to chairs, while a man in a white lab coat prepared a hypodermic needle and the masked man looked on with keen interest.

After abandoning the blimp in Topeka the entire party, captors and captives, had boarded a converted school bus painted gaudily with the graffiti of the day and leisurely motored to the commune.

Getting through the innumerable roadblocks set up by the Operation Quaker Snatchback high command had proved ridiculously simple. The veep and the two military men had been hidden in a secret compartment in the rear of the bus, while the drugged president had not been allowed to shave for three days and in his newly donned Levi's, Arlo Guthrie floppy hat and four-foot beard appeared to the police as just another stone-souled, thoroughly out of it, hirsute freak.

"I must know what this country's position is on the PEPPER talks, Dr. Street. You know how valuable that is to my overall strategy," the masked man said.

"This injection should unlock his psyche a bit," the doctor retorted, and hit the vein. The president's eyes rolled up, he sighed, and his head fell to one side.

"What? Needling the Number One of the nation with diabolical drugs?" the vice president protested.

The masked man snarled. "This one you can knock out completely... and with a rock if you want. He has nothing to offer but those endless alliterations." The doctor grinned and put the veep to sleep with another injection.

They waited expectantly for a response from the president. "Mr. President, what are you thinking about now?"

And then the president of the United States, a man whose mind held the innermost secrets on earth, opened his mouth. He began to sing: "Hail to the Redskins... Oh, charge on down the field..."

He cut the song short and a peeved look came over him, adding nothing endearing to a face already covered with permanent scowls. "Why doesn't George Allen use the plays I call in every week? That halfback pass option is a beauty. No wonder he lost the Superbowl."

"This is what is on his mind?" the masked man said quizzically.

"We've just prised off the top layer of his subconscious," the doctor said. "It'll take time. He's a deep one."

"Charisma... they say I have no charisma," the president said. "Charisma my foot. What do they want, a president or Neil Diamond?"

"We've hit the resentment layer, I think," the doctor noted. "Shouldn't be too far now from the secret section."

"Jane... Jane Fonda. I loved you in *Klute,* you in that black leather hooker outfit with all those tricks paying you one hundred dollars a night."

"All right," said the masked man. "What position will the United States take vis-a-vis Russia and China in the PEPPER talks? What compromises are you willing to make on Korea, Laos, Cambodia... ?"

"Why can't they cut their hair, damn 'em! In addition to looking grotesque they've killed the whole barber industry. I know... when I get back to Washington I'll jam through a twice-a-week haircutting bill... get 'em right by the short hairs... get the barber vote back."

"We are getting nowhere," the masked man said, quite annoyed.

"So what if *LIFE Magazine* went under? They never took good pictures of me."

"I am afraid," said the doctor, "that this is all we'll get for this session. He's sinking into a stupor."

"Perhaps I can obtain it from an even better source, the one man in the government who truly is informed." He lifted up a walkie-talkie and made a quick coded call.

SEVEN

While the intimate coterie privy to the shocking crime burned the midnight oil in a dozen offices, Washington, D.C. hummed along at its usual high-gear social whirl, unaware of the monstrous plot that threatened to shake the very foundations of democracy. At a glittering cocktail party in Georgetown some aerospace lobbyists, over glasses of Cold Duck, concluded a deal with the Justice Department by which a damaging indictment would be pigeon-holed in return for the unlisted phone numbers of the Golddiggers.

At RFK Stadium 50,000 baseball fans were whooping it up for the first time in many decades. After years of suffering with the cellar-dwelling Washington Senators they finally had a good reason to go to the ball park. The team had been shifted to Texas, and although the national pasttime was no more in the nation's Capital, season ticket sales were at an all-time high. The very notion of going to the stadium and not seeing a scoreboard reading MINNESOTA 12, NATS 0, or men letting pop flies drop with the bases loaded was too attractive to let go by. Now they luxuriated in their seats, ate their hot dogs, sipped their Carling Black Label and found it more intriguing to watch an old grounds keeper watering the Astroturf.

At the newly constructed Kennedy Center for the Performing Arts, Leonard Bernstein was conducting the Hall Johnson Choir in the stirring finale to an evening of Negro folk music. This selection was to the tune of the immortal classic, "Waterboy," whose new lyrics found special favor in the scandal-racked capital.

> *"Watergate...*
> *Where is it hidin'?*
> *If you doan watch out...*
> *Dey gonna bug yo' mammy...*
> *Dere ain't no squawkin'*
> *Or intimate talkin',*
> *Dat ain't overheard, boys...*
> *Dat ain't overheard...*
>
> *Each time yo' whistlin',*

De GOP's listenin',
So keep yo' big mouth shut,
Cause mum is de word..."

In that selfsame Watergate apartment complex about which had swirled the election controversy, the usual nightly activities were in sway. Senator Ribicoff, coin collection box in hand, was going from door to door asking for funds for the United Jewish Appeal. Two Congressmen were in the community laundry room, sharing a box of Tide and rinsing out secret documents. In the Safeway Supermarket, a vital part of the complex, the manager was closing up shop, putting the day's cash receipts in the meat cooler and the more valuable steaks and chops in the wall safe.

And in a Penthouse suite Dr. Henry Kissingherr leaned back on his divan, loosened his tie and now that he was in the privacy of his quarters let go the sigh he had not dared emit in the company of all those august intelligence chieftains: *"Oy vay is mir! Are we in trouble!"*

He kicked off his Florsheim shoes, then feeling the pangs of hunger decided to make himself his usual bedtime snack, an omelet, but fearful of what cholesterol might do to his already bulbous waistline he cracked open a dozen eggs and, as was his wont, skillfully culled the yolks and fried only the whites. He disposed of the yolks in the usual way, hurling them violently against a large canvas on the living room wall. There they quickly adhered to thousands of other long-since-dried egg yolks to create a fascinating abstract painting, "Sunburst," which he led visitors to believe was a rare example of early Picasso in his Yellow Period.

He wolfed down his simple repast, placed Beethoven's *Eroica* on his stereo and between sips of Diet Dr. Pepper gazed upon a wall laden with the many photos he had taken with world leaders. There he was with Mao opening a fortune cookie, there with Golda Meir (also opening a fortune cookie, for long had the Jewish nation kept the Chinese food industry from going under), with DeGaulle, shaded from the brilliant Parisian sun by the general's generous nose, with Willy Brandt, Brezhnev, Tanaka, Sinatra, any world leader one could think of.

About to catch forty winks he eased his ponderous frame onto the bed, but noticed a brown paper package tied with a single string lying on it. Ach, goot, his shirts were back from the laundry. But why had they been left there and not put into his dresser? Unforgivable negligence! One more slip such as this and housekeeper Heidi would be back in front of her old stand in Manhattan's Yorkville selling hot chestnuts and bratwurst.

Then the owlish eyes narrowed. There was a ticket tucked into the cross tie: "Humble thanks for your most honorable patronage—The Ming Around the Collar Chinese Laundry."

He had never sent his shirts to such an establishment before. Usually his things were tossed in with the White House laundry and then brought to his suite. In that instant Dr. Kissingherr knew a contact had been made. He ripped off the string, thumbed through the shirts and there on the cardboard in the neck of the bottom shirt he found it, a note written in the ornate calligraphy of a Mandarin scribe:

> *"Confucius once said, 'Show me intoxicated warlord without false teeth and I will show you a gummy rummy.' He who would know more of the wisdom of Confucius and, incidentally, information concerning personage of high rank spirited away in a blimp would do well to be at the intersection of the Street of the Cruddy Carp and the Alley of the Moulting Maggot in Peking at sunset on the morrow. By the way, Herr Kissingherr, we hope we did not put too much starch in your Van Heusen."*

Deciding rapidly to follow this first, albeit slim, lead, he dressed quickly and telephoned an unlisted number. "It'll be ready, sir, on a moment's notice," the terse voice said and hung up.

Incredible, he thought. The Chinese linked to this plot? After the president's successful visit and a new dawn for Sino-American relations?

Had the Maoist regime been deposed by counterrevolutionaries? Were the Red Guards raging out of control again? And, most importantly, was the sweet and pungent pork at the Marco Polo takeout restaurant still rated No. 1 by Duncan Hines?

The answers to these burning questions would be found in the inscrutable Orient, Dr. Henry Kissingherr's next port of call.

EIGHT

The supersonic air force jet came to rest on the tarmac of Peking Airport, and Dr. Kissingherr made his way quickly past a receiving line of Chicom officials, who, if surprised by his sudden visit, discreetly made no inquiries. In making his request for entry into Red China he had used a typical cover story about a romantic involvement, in this case a young pretty interpreter who, he admitted to Chou-En-Lai, had been "a great ball at the Great Wall." Knowing his amorous predilections they had bought it.

Although sunset was nigh, the doctor did notice in the waning rays that China had undergone a vast change since he had paved the way for its reentry into the family of nations by his daring diplomatic coup in 1972. Already Westernization was beginning to set in, and from his vantage point at the intersection stipulated in the message, he could see a theater marquee flashing the appearance of *Clockwork Mandarin Orange*, nearby kiosks whose sole product formerly was *The Thoughts of Chairman Mao*, now carrying such paperback titles as *Jonathan Mao Seagull, The Mao-Father, The Sensuous Chairman,* and so forth.

Working his chopsticks into a dish he had purchased from a street vendor, he thought, I could really get hooked on this Chinese food, become a regular chow mein-liner, and chuckled at his witty pun.

Precisely at sundown there was a soft whisper, "Dr. Kissingherr?" and he looked through the curtains of a Yellow Pedicab which had just pulled over.

He nodded, *"Ja,"* and followed the beckoning hand inside. He found himself seated next to a sensationally formed Chinese maiden, whose willowy limbs peeked provocatively through the slit in her cheongsam. At a burst of Chinese from the girl, the sweating scrawny man pulling the device lifted up his harness, she dumped a handful of hot steaming rice into his eager mouth and he pulled them away with renewed vigor.

"We get forty-five miles to the bowl," she smiled. "Fifty if he's on the open road." She lit a Shansei cigarette, puffed out a sensuous curl of smoke and said coolly, "Welcome to China, Herr Doktor. I am your contact, Wu Wu, an odd name for a Chinese, but my father was a great fan of the late movie comedian Hugh

Hubert. Woo... woo... woo-woo," and as she repeated the mindless phrase her eyes began to roll, a maniacal grin appeared on her face and her fingers fluttered.

"The clinic of Dr. Ling Ah Ling—and chop-chop!" she commanded the pedicab puller. "I am sure you have many questions to ask, but I shall let Dr. Ling answer them. Would you care for some refreshments perhaps, some water chestnuts, some succulent bamboo shoots, some sweet and sour crickets?"

The doctor, realizing this archaic mode of transportation might take some time, began to study his companion more closely and saw that in addition to the finely turned calves there were two Himalayan breasts jutting out of the brocaded blouse and viewing them in all their thrusting glory he found a catchy little refrain from an American television commercial running through his head: *Everybody needs milk.* He was also aware that the very sound of her name, Wu Wu, (woo-woo) meant love-love, and such a diversion might be welcome, indeed, for who knew how long the driver would be chop-chopping? But, alas, the words of love did not come easily to this sensitive, shy man and so he began to make some rather banal, time-consuming conversation.

"Do you know," he said mildly, "the annual production of manganese in Southeast Asia has nearly quadrupled in the last decade?"

She blushed and suddenly her almond eyes, which had been so cool and contained, were now drooping demurely and he realized, be they Oriental or Occidental, his brand of diplomatic pornography had the power to hit home.

"And that the hardy new strain of rice developed by American agronomists has nearly doubled the acreage in the Phillipines?"

She began to squirm, hating herself for this display of blatant emotionalism so alien to her

Oriental makeup, but strangely loving it as well.

"Oh, Doctor," she said in a small voice. "Tell me more "

The owlish eyes narrowed, the lips puckered and said, "The coming food of the future is..." and he whispered seductively... "kelp!"

"Oh, Henry, you foreign devil... you're driving me mad!" And now the peach yellow of her skin was invaded by a rosy flush, her breasts liberated themselves with a heave that sent the buttons flying. Of its own accord the slit on her cheongsam ripped a pathway to her arms, and to insure there would be no interruption of this moment of fulfillment she reached into her purse, extracted another bowlful of hot rice, flung it into the driver's face and let herself surrender to this unique Caucasian with his strange, yet effective, verbal gift.

Their joint climax came somewhere between his brilliant explanation of the Boxer Rebellion of 1895 and the Long March of the Red Army, though he managed to extend the moment of orgasm with a quick improvised digest of the events leading to the overthrow of Fulgencia Battista.

The interlude finished, he leaned back, spent a profitable five minutes scribbling a report on the possible effects of a one-megaton nuclear explosion in Lake Erie (would this be a cheap way of cleansing this polluted waterway, he thought, and would there be any significant repercussions from the bombed-out population of Cleveland?), when the slap-slap-slap of the coolie pedicab puller's naked feet suddenly began to slow. He pushed aside the shade and noted they were now somewhere outside the city limits. The setting was rural, sparsely populated, containing tormented, wind-twisted trees and dingy huts. Typical old China, he thought, but there was an exception—a gleaming one-story modern building drastically at variance with the ancient surroundings.

"We are here," Wu Wu said, and stepped onto a tiled walkway leading to the front entrance.

With his usual elan the doctor pressed a one hundred-sen tip into the panting coolie's bony hand and another gift as well. "Here, my man, an autographed copy of my latest hardcover book, *The Uses of Treachery in Diplomacy*."

The coolie bowed obsequiously and felt the pages of the volume. Not bad, he thought. Much softer than rice paper and though it did not come in rolls he and his family would put it to the best of use.

Dr. Kissingherr followed the clacking heels down the tileway, a sense of excitement surging through his drip-dry suit; here was the first opportunity to grab a piece of the puzzle.

A door hummed open electronically and he found himself inside what appeared to be a reception room to a doctor's office. It was plushly carpeted, lit by modernistic lamps, and containing, like doctor's offices all over the world, a sign in Chinese which he translated: UNLESS YOU HAVE MADE PRIOR ARRANGEMENTS, ALL VISITS REQUIRE PAYMENT IN CASH.

"Ah, Dr. Kissingherr! This is the privilege of a lifetime, sir." The speaker was Chinese, plump, modly dressed, the eyes shrewd and penetrating, the accent impeccable Cambridge. "I am Dr. Ling Ah Ling, so named because my father spent some time in your adopted country, had an affair with an Avon lady..."

"Yes, the name Ling Ah Ling does ring a bell. 'Avon balling,'" the presidential aide quipped. "Precisely," his host smiled.

"I must be frank with you, Dr. Ling. Time is of the essence in this extremely delicate matter. I assume that you did not put a message into my laundry for a jest. Where is the august personage alluded to in your missive?"

The joviality left the face of the Chinese who, linking his arm with that of the presidential agent, steered the latter into an inner office. Another electronic door opened and shut, but not before the visitor caught a final glance at the girl's face and saw it taut with tension, then felt a chill in his own body. What had he gotten into in this Godforsaken place in the wilds of China where no one knew where he was? In his zeal to crack this case had he blundered?

Four muscular arms locking his body in a viselike grip, four hard eyes and a smirk on the face of Dr. Ling Ah Ling told him he had, indeed.

He was pressed quickly onto a table, manacled to cuffs on the ends of chains, while Dr. Ling, with a cavalier look, lit a Cavalier cigarette and cavalierly blew a stream of smoke into his face, "Thank heaven, I'm not smoking Lucky Strike or this shtick would never work."

"It appears I have made a mistake, *ja?*" Dr. Kissingherr said, manifesting his coolness. "I lave violated Clawsewitz's first principle and recklessly charged in without first solidifying my base of operations."

"Indeed you have," Dr. Ling said, "but now I want information fast. Since we have as yet been unable to obtain the U.S. position on PEPPER from your hard-to-break-down commander in chief I want it from you... now."

"I will never betray my trust."

Something metallic gleamed in Dr. Ling's right hand. "This, my friend, is an acupuncture needle, the symbol of my trade, for I am the acknowledged acupuncturist in the field.

I have used needles like this to miraculously cure thousands of patients of pain that your Western doctors could not cope with. Upon occasion I have also used them to knit an adorable cuddly sweater. Tonight, if you do not cooperate, they will be the instrumentation of your doom."

At a snap of his fingers the two tall Chinese goons stripped off Dr. Kissingherr's garments, leaving him a quivering naked mound of paunchy fear.

"As you know, mein Herr Doktor, when placed in various parts of the body, acupuncture needles can block pain-producing nerves. When placed in other anatomical locations they produce paralysis throughout the total physiognomy and if not extracted in time cause all the functions to halt and bring on inevitable death."

He thrust out with the needle; Dr. Kissingherr felt the slightest of pricks, then a loss of feeling in his left arm. Dr. Ling chuckled, "Soon, you will be the world's most glorified pincushion." Another needle found its mark, then another and another and in a minute he had lost virtually all feeling in the right side of his body.

"Again, the U.S. position, Dr. Kissingherr?"

The prisoner refused to speak.

"As the immortal Sherlock Holmes was wont to say to his biographer, 'Quick, Watson, the needle!' " The thugs pressed another batch of needles into Dr. Ling's fingers and with a few more deft placements Dr. Kissingherr's left side was now paralyzed.

"For the last time, will you tell me what I wish to know?"

Dr. Kissingherr opened his lips and spoke through mounting pain, and the Chinese doctor put his ear to that tortured mouth, confident he had at last cracked the shell of courage of his world-famous captive.

"It may be all over for me, Dr. Ling, but it doesn't matter because back home there are a million guys named Kowalski, Smith, Greenberg, O'Hara, Nelson, MacTavish, and Carver who'll be coming after you in B-17s, P-40s, and Liberty ships. Yeah, you dirty Japs started this war, but a hundred million Yanks will finish it!"

Dr. Ling's eyes popped in surprise. He had expected to hear top-secret information and instead had been barraged by Dana Andrews's fiery speech from the World War II movie, *The Purple*

Heart. It was clear Kissingherr was too far gone to be of any further use.

"The rest of the needles," he ordered his subordinates. Now he abandoned all medical finesse and was flinging them in like a dart champion at a Polish Falcons club in Trenton, New Jersey. In they bit, point after point after point. "Match point," sneered Dr. Ling. "You are now virtually immobile."

"But I can still talk," the diplomat said in wonder.

"Yes, I have left the vocal area unimpaired. It will delight me to know that the great Henry Kissingherr, a man whose voice has moved prime ministers and kings, is screaming his head off like some helpless child. *Auf wiedersehen,* Herr Doktor."

So this is to be my inglorious end, Henry Kissingherr thought sardonically. I had hoped that when the final curtain went down it would not have been the Bamboo Curtain of Red China, but at least rocking my way out in the waterbed of a bit player from Twentieth Century Fox. But here I am on a cold table in a maniac's acupuncture clinic, looking for all the world like some giant porcupine.

"If I am to die, at least tell me, what part are you playing in this global cabal?"

"It would do you no good to know who the Mr. Big is in this operation, Herr Doktor. All you need to know is that in one hour you will be a dead man."

He blew a last jet of smoke into the stricken man's face and, trailed by his agents, walked out of sight.

The glare of the overhead light caused Kissingherr's still movable eyes to squint. To avoid its assault he shifted them slightly and in doing so noticed that a rear window of the clinic was partially open, allowing a bit of the cold night air to swirl in. Yes, he thought again, here I am just a pincushion waiting for the moments to tick away. And how many were left now? Fifty-five minutes? Fifty-four? Fifty-three... ?

What good is owning the world's most fantastic brain now that I lie here on a table, pierced in a thousand places, my life functions waning away? What good is all the studying I did from my birth, nay, even before birth, when this insuperable mind of mine was able to memorize all the internal parts of a woman's body as I lay in Momma's womb?

Ah, Momma, I remember Momma. That day in May, 1923, when I came into existence in Fertz, Bavaria. Ah, my beloved

Fertz. The very name has an air to it. Ach, Momma was such a good cook, her chicken dumplings light as feathers—in those hard days of post-World War I Germany sometimes made *of* feathers—her knaidlach, knishes, knockwurst (if it started with "kn" Momma could make it). And Poppa, gentle, polite, good-natured, a school teacher respected by all. And between the two of them, always the urging, "Heinz"—he smiled at the memory of his old name, anglicized to Henry when they blessedly had escaped the murderous Third Reich—"Heinz, learn my child, learn. Knowledge is the tool by which you will achieve your goal."

So they had given him a complete set of the *Encyclopedia Britannica* at age three. To further stimulate his desire to learn, Momma and Poppa had used an old Jewish trick; they had sweetened each page of the massive *Britannica* set with honey so that he could lick it off as an incentive to reading and learning. By the time he was four he had tongued his way from *A* to *Z* into staggering knowledge and overweight.

But what in those volumes could save him now, as he looked for all the world like a German-Jewish porcupine?

Wait! What was that nonsensical simile? A German-Jewish porcupine!

And suddenly his encyclopedic mind was riffling through the pages of the *Britannica* for something buried deep. What was it? Aardvark? Atom bomb? No. He let his mind skip like a stone over water through cookie cutter, dinosaur, Haleloki... strange what images were popping up in his journey through the alphabet. Kilarney... and what in God's name was he fixating on Kilarney for? Latvia, lemming, laxative, Manet, Manischewitz (which made far more sense than Kilarney). The *P*s... Pennsylvania, Polly Adler (the famed Jewish madam, who no matter what else had been said about her, at least she kept a Kosher house). And then he struck the gold his mind had been panning for so frantically. He squeezed his eyes and the words appeared, the words that could give a one in a million chance of freeing himself from this hideous ordeal. Dr. Kissingherr pursed his lips and emitted a throbbing low whistle.

NINE

It had been a lonely, loveless twelve months for T'su. Although the rest of the Chinese world was celebrating the Year of the Ox, for T'su it had been the Year of the Strikeout and if this condition prevailed an ox would start to look good. For 365 days he had gone without the warm sweetness of fulfilled sensuality. Though he had combed the hills and brush for a mate, there had been none available to slake his lust. Under ordinary circumstances he would have wondered to himself: Is my deodorant letting me down? My mouthwash? My cologne? But these were not ordinary circumstances and T'su no ordinary unrequited lover, because the sex-starved creature waddling through the night was a porcupine.

Yes, he had known fantasies. Once in a feverish haze he had mistaken a wind-blown spiny shrub for a member of the opposite sex and followed for nearly a mile whispering hot porcupine entreaties, "Oh, baby! Quill me! Stick me!" And just when he was about to make his amorous move the objection of his affection had been eaten right in front of his eyes by a goat. Only yesterday he had thrown caution to the winds and tried to molest a bramble bush. So it was in a grumpy mood that T'su poked under rocks and leaves, hoping to find his heart's desire, but drawing a stinging slap in the snout from the whipping tail of a beaver and the snide comment, "Get your paws off me, queer!"

Ah yes, the rejected creature thought with bitterness. Johnny Cash was right. *Life ain't easy for a porcupine named T'su.*

The throbbing whistle wafting on the breeze pierced his dark mood and he suddenly froze. Was this another fantasy mocking him? His mind playing more cruel tricks? But no, it was beyond doubt the sexually inspired whistle of a female in heat and he felt a chill in every quill, a shiver in each quiver, and a sensation so divine in every spine.

But where was the source of his concupiscence emanating from? It seemed to be from a window in the one-story building only a few yards away and he asked himself: is it possible that something in that strange man-made edifice holds promise for me? No, I must be going mad. But the whistle, insistent and provocative, kept drawing him closer. I'll take a chance, he thought, this is no time to hedgehog my bets, making a porcupine pun.

With a great leap he hurled his bristling body through the window, sending the pane flying into a thousand sharp shards, and when a few of them penetrated his body he thought, oh, baby, what crazy foreplay!

He landed on all fours on the tiled floor and his eyes bulged at the glorious sight before them.

A creature was lying on a table, covered with hundreds and hundreds of shiny silver needles, each winking in the light. T'su thought, Oh, my God, the drought is over! What an Amazonian beauty! If there was a Las Vegas for porcupines surely this one would be dancing in center stage at the Lido!

A thrill of equal dimensions sped through Dr. Kissingherr as his eyes saw the drooling intruder stalking toward him, a definite manifestation of erectility sliding from only heaven knew where in that cactuslike body. The Kissingherr mind had done it again, his cerebral perusal of the encyclopedia had given him that million-to-one shot. Would it pay off?

Immediately he knew along what lines he must proceed and it would have to be quick, for the porcupine's premature ejaculation would ruin his entire plan. As seductively as he could—considering the nature of his new companion—the doctor breathed in Chinese:

"Love me, love me..."

T'su scrambled up on the table, his eyes glazed with a red lust, and, to prolong the moment he had so long dreamed of, took one of the shiny needles in his mouth and lovingly worked his lips over it, giving it little bites and tugs, until finally it fell out of the punctured skin, immediately restoring movement to that portion it had paralyzed.

"Encore, encore," Dr. Kissingherr panted, and the porcupine, seeing it had turned on its outsized lover, bent its head and continued its oral ministrations on a second needle, yanking it free, then a third, a fourth.

"More, more," the beneedled figure pleaded. "I love it and I love you!" and then T'su went completely mad, sucking and tugging, until the needles were piling up on the floor in a glittering mound. With each freed needle, the presidential superagent felt movement restored and now he was in a position to yank out the remaining ones and also to jump from the table and elude the sex-mad creature that was hot on his tail. With a final shiver, T'su experienced the sensation he had long been seeking and fell into a crumpled ball of contentment.

Now the doctor felt the body-wide tingling of a man reborn. He slipped quickly into his drip-dry suit and regimental tie and sat down to figure out his next move. Here he was in the middle of nowhere, the near-victim of a murder plot and yet he was no closer to solving this mystery, and the PEPPER talks were twenty-four hours nearer. Who was Dr. Ling Ah Ling and how was he tied to this conspiracy?

The owlish eyes darted around the room, almost empty save for the table and lamp. But wait! In a corner was a filing cabinet, obviously crammed with Dr. Ling's cases. He slid the drawers open and rummaged through the contents, folders of acupuncture patients, each containing charts, X-rays, case histories and in a few the wry notations: "Deadbeat. Must pay in advance." Or, "Send to collection agency."

Nothing here, he thought, but then in the rear of the drawer he found an eight-by-ten glossy... depicting twenty nude bodies intertwined in various acts of love and a twenty-first individual, fully clad, preparing sandwiches. Ach, what hardcore pornography, he thought, and how has it found its way to this land of classical culture? Dr. Ling must have some odd Western tastes. Then one of the faces in the mass group-grope seemed to leap out at him. It was the girl, Wu Wu, his paramour of the pedicab, the maiden who led him into this trap. He flipped it over and on the back were stamped the letters: PORNOCAT PRODUCTIONS, SAN FRANCISCO.

Obviously, he thought with his usual clarity, one of those Bay Area film firms devoted to grinding out the type of salacious material so shocking to the millions of Americans who lined up in front of theaters every week to see it.

Well, it was a slender thread at best, but with so much at stake one worth pursuing. Once outside the clinic he hailed a passing Checker Pedicab and made his way back to the airport. The U.S. jet was waiting for him and soon the blue Pacific was in view. He sighed, considering what fates lay ahead at his next port of call. If these people had gone to such extreme lengths to destroy him in China, it was quite conceivable that new horrors were in the offing and that he might, indeed, leave his heart in San Francisco... and maybe the good parts as well.

TEN

Darkness over Mount Rushmore... the figure on the packmule climbing to the clifftop... smashing, pounding, laughing insanely again... another night of hell for the four granite immortals whose faces were becoming wearier and wearier with each foray.

"Soon, soon," the man on the rope whispered to the wind. "Soon..." And Washington, patriot though he was, could not check a traitorous thought: If only the British had won; then Cornwallis would be taking this crap every night...

ELEVEN

As the plane bearing Dr. Kissingherr dipped low to salute the city by the Bay, he could see gleaming in the first rays of the sun the immortal Golden Gate Bridge, a span which had once been the longest in the world. Underneath its graceful lines had passed myriads of U.S. Navy craft heading to and from war, and its towering height had made San Francisco the acknowledged suicide capital of the world. Even as the plane crossed the bridge on its pass toward International Airport he could see hundreds of people queuing up for their demise, taking numbers off racks to assure an orderly succession of final plunges, and nearby to service the would-be suicides were the various businesses catering to their special needs—lawyers sitting at tables making out last wills and testaments, beauticians and manicurists grooming the plungers so that they would not look slovenly when their bloated bodies were fished out of the water, clergymen of various denominations giving them final succor and the Mark Shpritz School of Diving and Swimming, a recently organized franchise which had units on every major span in the country to teach the suicides how to hit the water with class.

Circling in he could also spot the city's most revered shrine, the fifty-foot statue of Tony Bennett, adored by the citizenry for his remarkable song that had put this city on the map. Hundreds of pilgrims were foxtrotting at the base of the pedestal, and a host of other sights made this truly the Paris of the Pacific.

The CIA boys had provided him with a full dossier on Pornocat Productions, the details of which were already snapped by the camera of his mind. The company had started in the freewheeling, barrier-breaking sexual revolution of the 1960s, with a series of sixteen-millimeter films shot for a few hundred dollars in seamy apartment houses, saving precious money by letting the landlords watch—and frequently join in. The early scripts had been rather rudimentary affairs, with little dialogue, calling for a knock at the door, the appearance of a repairman and some labored excuse for the lonely housewife to somehow divest herself of her clothing while he was fiddling at the back of her Norge, sometimes her Frigidaire. These affairs generally culminated in a scene with two naked bodies thrashing on a bed while milk soured and broccoli wilted in the unrepaired icebox.

They had brought in enough money to allow the filmmakers to let their creative energies run rampant. Now these flicks were done in Technicolor, quadrophonic sound, with the best lighting, technicians, professional directors, and scriptwriters purveying a polished product in which a repairman knocked at the door, a housewife found some excuse to get undressed while he was titillating her Kelvinator and running amok over her Amana.

The brain behind Pornocat was a six-foot-ten black, streetwise giant named Rafer Raper. If he had been funnier, he might have been another Bill Cosby, more limber, he might have been pouring in thirty-two points a night for the Baltimore Bullets, but being neither he drew upon his basic strength—an ability to carry on intercourse for hours at a clip. Beginning with minor roles in porno films he soon achieved star status and was named in 1966 at the National Academy for Pornographic Pictures as the actor of the year. The *Los Angeles Free Press,* which had covered the prestigious banquet, noted that Raper, when given their equivalent of the Oscar (The Peter) was bigger where it mattered than the statuette itself.

Not to be outdone by the Paul Newmans and Steve McQueens, he, too, formed his own production company and parlayed it into a multimillion dollar a year business, which had achieved such legitimacy that it had been accepted on the New York Stock Exchange. In short, it had gone pubic. And it had also garnered for the giant a mansion on Nob Hill, at whose door Dr. Kissingherr now stood.

But not in his old recognizable form in the drip-dry suit, regimental tie and omnipresent attache case. The new Herr Doktor had been garbed by his intelligence cohorts in nail-studded, flare-bottomed Levi's, a ratty San Quentin prisoner's jacket, workboots, and as an added touch of contemporaneity even his tongue was covered with a thin layer of faded blue denim, for he had learned from his China experience that a solid cover was mandatory.

He pressed a pudgy finger into what he took to be the doorbell, but instead of the customary cheery chimes he was greeted by a prerecorded trailing sigh, a quick moan and an anxious voice asking, "Did it happen for you, too?" The door opened. "Yes?" came from the full pouting lips of a ravishing

Nordic blonde in silver lamé hot pants, knee-high boots and a copper pendant that bounced from breast to breast.

"I have an appointment with Mr. Raper. Will you please tell him that Eric Von Blowheim, the prominent European pornographer, has arrived." Giving him a friendly bite on the ear, she led him past a series of rooms all ablaze with lights, whirring cameras and a kind of assembly-line productivity that would have made General Motors proud.

Supple young actresses performing Olympian contortions moved from scene to scene, receiving a bite here, a penetration there. Here was a trio which had gone past the sexual number 69 and into 207; four people cavorted under a driving shower; six on a water bed; three on a match. One young man twisted free of a twenty-two person orgy to go to the men's room and to assure himself he would find his place upon his return he left a bookmark.

If all involved had by some miracle managed to reach simultaneous climaxes the energy expended would have widened the San Andreas Fault by one hundred feet and sent San Francisco sliding into Sausalito.

Viewing the entire operation from his throne, a look of professional detachment on his face, was the man Dr. Kissingherr had come to probe, Rafer Raper himself, a Watusi in a floor-length sable bathrobe that covered a diamond-speckled safari suit. Grouped about him were adoring females of various hues and sizes, all curvaceous and breasty, hanging on his every word and what ever else was available. And suddenly Dr. Kissingherr's heart gave a jump. There, ensconced among them, was the Chinese girl, Wu Wu, who had led him into the near catastrophe at the clinic.

Rafer Raper's eyes flickered interestedly at the newcomer. "So you the kraut dude who got a hot new screenplay for me, huh?"

Dr. Kissingherr placed the scenario into the pinkish palm. He had ordered the CIA to set up an interview with Raper, decided on his cover as a foreign porno filmmaker and requested they have a manuscript ready for presentation. Because there had been little time to create an original screenplay, three security boys grabbed the first handy book off the shelf, which happened to be a Mark Twain classic, and batted out an X-rated version.

"Love the title already—*Huckleberry Fuck*" the giant grinned, glancing at the cover. "What's it about?"

"Well, it concerns a freckle-faced urchin who travels the Mississippi, going down on a raft..."

"A marvelous new use of oral sex," Raper said in approval. "I'll get six chicks to play the raft. Great! I'll buy it sight unseen." He pressed a roll of thousand-dollar bills into the doctor's hand.

"Hey, Von Blowheim, you look like you really into the nitty-gritty. You get started like I did, makin' beaver films?"

"Ach, *nein*. Beavers hold no interest for me. I have always preferred to photograph human beings."

"No, man. I don't mean beavers. I mean *beavers*."

"That is what I mean," the doctor said in mild reproof. "Let the Disney people film beavers. As I said, I would rather capture the sexual habits of people."

The black man's eyes became two ice cubes, his mouth a tight slit as a bulb went off in his brain. This kraut would have to be checked out fast, but he let his usual grin return and put an arm around the visitor's shoulder. "Why don't you join in the orgy? Find a chick and take your pick. It isn't often I have such a distinguished continental visitor."

"I find the Chinese girl particularly attractive."

The giant waved his hand and Wu Wu obediently undulated into the doctor's arms. Good, he exulted inwardly; there would be an opportunity to question her.

She led him into a room lit dimly by a yellow lava lamp, two great balls of plastic floating in a thick transparent liquid. To the designer these spheres must have suggested the cosmos constantly uniting and breaking away as though to create a new solar system. To the doctor, however, with his Hebraic frame of reference, they looked like two matzoh balls mating. Wu Wu drew him down upon a clutch of scattered throw pillows.

Well, he thought, I suppose it is necessary to go through with this sexual charade, although with time whizzing by I would much rather get to the interrogation, but I cannot let her know who I am as yet. I will have to play it by ear... or, more fittingly, by rear, considering the nature of this place. "I find you fascinating," he said woodenly.

Oh no, she thought, another deadhead. This man has all the magnetism of a boxboy at an Alpha Beta food market. If it weren't for Raper I'd give this overstuffed sausage the bum's rush.

Sensing her indifference he pushed on. "You are exciting, tantalizing, captivating."

She yawned. It's like listening to Ovaltine, she thought.

His spirit dampened. Here was the quarry he had been seeking and already he was facing rejection. He could not lose her now. Grasping at mental straws, he moved in closer, clutched her hands and whispered, "Though it was not impeccable, the Marshall Plan at least had the virtue of rebuilding the devastated heavy industries of war-torn Europe."

The sullen aloofness on her face was driven off by a wave of sudden interest. "Pray, do go on..."

"Shortly thereafter Tito made his historic break with hardline Communism and pressed forward with his revisionist brand, evoking the undying wrath of Stalin, who manifested his displeasure by massing a million troops on the Yugoslavian border and banning the sale of Nat King Cole records in Moscow."

"Oh." Her hand flew to her throat now tight with the hot feeling of *deja vu*. Where had she been turned on before by a soft, low purring voice spewing out this erotica? Where?

"Washington quickly seized the opportunity and drove a wedge into the Communist monolith." Now the wave of sudden interest had fled the lovely Oriental face to be supplanted by a look of seething sexuality and the fine arms were drawing him close to her. "Oh, Henry, I knew it was you!" And before he could even hammer home the finishing blow, his explanation of the events leading to the dismissal of MacArthur by Truman, she was his, her lips crushing the words "Yalu River" back into his mouth as she used her Asian pillow-book techniques to steer him into a crashing climax.

"You must tell me where that certain person is, Wu Wu. Why did Dr. Ling try to have me killed? Who is pulling the strings?"

In an inner office Rafer Raper lifted his gold cocaine spoon and snorted an ounce into a broad nostril. That clinched it... that diplomatic gobbledegook and her sigh of "Oh, Henry." Then there was that asinine remark about beavers. What pornographer worth his saltpeter would not know that the term "beaver" referred to the female genitalia? So, Dr. Kissingherr himself had come into the lion's den and clearly was pulling the girl away from the conspiracy with his amatory technique. The situation called for a drastic resolution, but here was not the place to apply the finisher, too many people around, too messy.

"Henry," she said, casting wary glances about. "It's too dangerous to talk here. Meet me tomorrow at 9 A.M. at Hyde Street and we'll go for a cablecar ride. Then I'll tell you whatever I can."

Raper, his ear to the listening device, smiled wickedly. Then it would be tomorrow...

TWELVE

At precisely 9 A.M., after a refreshing sleep at the Fairmount Hotel and a delicious GOP breakfast special of ITT Shredded Paper with milk, sugar and some sort of fruit, Dr. Kissingherr stood at the top of Hyde Street, looking down at Fisherman's Wharf, some miles away. His need for disguise no longer necessary, he was back in his drip-dry suit and tie, and true to her word the maiden came into view, made a great show of trying to ignore him and stepped daintily into the rickety cablecar.

There were but two others on the vehicle, one a portly motorman in front, the other a rear brakeman, who, as the doctor and the girl boarded, were involved in a discussion about the previous night's presentation of *The Barber of Seville* at the San Francisco Opera House.

"Look, Lefty," the motorman snapped. "I don't give a shit what you say. To me the tenor, although facile in the high ranges, gave a thoroughly superficial performance without one insightful nuance into the libretto."

"Your ass!" the brakeman countered. "What the fuck do you know about opera? I say the tenor, albeit a trifle tentative in the early scenes, came to full flower, demonstrating fluidity in reaching the upper tonal register. He soared... I tell you the motherfucker soared!"

How magnificent to discover culture even among the city's lowborn, the doctor mused, but now it was time for the long delayed questioning. "We are alone, Wu Wu. Quickly..."

The girl lit one of her Shansei cigarettes and gazed thoughtfully as the car began to roll. "Dr. Ling Ah Ling is my father. Although he practices Marxism publicly, he is the leader of a dissident faction in China that wishes to place a descendant of the corrupt Dowager Empress back upon the throne, unseat the Mao regime, restore the opium trade, slavery, famine and the other outstanding attributes that made old China the citadel of culture it once was before the revolution. His task was to lure you to the clinic and eliminate you."

"Who recruited him into this affair?"

"Several weeks ago my father was contacted while on a visit to Hong Kong. He was told to go to the Caribbean island of Ronrico, a rum-producing nation, where he conferred with a group of other people drawn into this affair, a strange mixed bag of races and varying shades of political opinion. Apparently each was promised something for joining the cabal. Let me anticipate your next question by saying that the leader was not only masked but obviously a magnificent actor for he was able to function like a chameleon, changing his accent and dialect with each person he conversed with. Among those was my employer, Rafer Raper, who was there for reasons known only to him."

"*Liebschen*, how did you get into this sleazy porno business?"

"I was always starstruck, but the Chinese film industry was overly Marxist-oriented. There was no room for a girl who wanted to play sex symbols. The state-owned companies were grinding out dull propaganda films, with no opportunity for me to don enticing garments. The closest I ever got to recognition was in a film called *Production Is Rising* in which I played a tractor. Instead of an offer from United Artists, the best I got was one from International Harvester. So when Rafer Raper expressed interest in having me do his films, I leaped at the chance. Being violated by six men simultaneously is not my idea of *Camille*, but an artist must go where the work is."

The car was at Jackson Street, affording him a view of the beautiful yet terrifying downgrade they had yet to traverse. To take his mind off the precipitous hill that already was causing the butterflies in his stomach to jump back into their cocoons, he probed further.

"My dear, this is a vital matter. Was there anyone else at the meeting that your father might have mentioned?"

She thought hard. "I seem to recall that my father mentioned a rather unusual name... Monte Monte."

The presidential agent's ears pricked up. Monte Monte. Where had he heard that name? Something to do with television, perhaps.

Moving past Pacific Avenue down the steep descent toward Broadway, Dr. Kissingherr suddenly froze, for it seemed that the cablecar had picked up speed and, indeed, had rushed by some people waiting to board it at Vallejo Street. *Gott in Himmel,* he shuddered, and began to tremble even further because the faces of the conductor and brakeman had gone white, a particularly unusual circumstance for the former was Japanese and the latter Negro. "I can't stop it!" the brakeman screamed. "I think the cable's broken."

Or cut, Dr. Kissingherr quivered. They've gotten to me again through the girl. Dropping his politesse, he let go a string of long-forgotten, but suddenly recalled Yiddish invectives, the strongest of which had something to do with leaving a scatalogical souvenir in the ocean.

"Henry, I swear by the belly of the Buddha I had nothing to do with this!" she called out, but her words were lost in the wind rushing past the cablecar. Then a Cadillac came gunning down the hill at a rate which put it parallel to the out of control cablecar, a great ebony face leaned out the window and smirked, "Goodbye, traitor!" A hand squeezed the trigger of a silenced Luger and the girl fell into his lap, dead. More shots thudded and the conductor and brakeman, still at their posts in a vain effort to stem the plunge, doubled over and lay silent. "Goodbye, Mr. Kraut Dude. You on your own," Rafer Raper snarled and spun off into the next side street.

Now it was clear. He was on a juggernaut to doom, alone, his potential allies strewn in attitudes of death around him. He rushed to the rear and started pulling down at the brake, but it was hopeless. Somehow, the kingpin pornographer had arranged to sever the underground cable that held the car to the tracks and the brake was a useless, dead instrument.

As always in moments of dire peril, his life flashed before him... or tried to... but by the time the plummeting cablecar got to Union Street, leaving the life more than a block behind, the life called out, "Henry, I can't keep up!"

He thought of jumping but shrank back, for now the tracks seemed to be two silver blurs in front of him, and to abandon the car now would merely leave him a smashed-up drip-dry suit and a mangled attache case.

Ach, looming in front of him was a truck coming across Greenwich Street, the letters "IRONSIDE —AN NBC-TV PRODUCTION" across its sides, obviously in the midst of filming a segment of the famous show about the wheelchair-bound police chief of Frisco. Just as the cablecar reached the truck, Raymond Burr wheeled out, cringed at the onrushing car, but could not wheel himself back into the truck. A side of the cablecar rammed the actor's chair and suddenly he too was rolling madly down the long hill toward Fisherman's Wharf, crying out, "And for this I gave up 'Perry Mason'?". But the doctor sighed with relief when he saw the bulky Burr dive out of the chair into a parade of Shriners crossing Lombard Street. They cheerfully caught Burr, gave him a drink from a flask, popped a fez on his head and continued across the street in pursuit of three teenage drum majorettes they had been trailing since they left the St. Francis Hotel.

Gottsedanken, Burr is safe, but what about me? the doctor thought. My president is a prisoner of a masked madman, a beautiful Chinese pornographic film star lies dead at my feet, I am rocketing to my doom on a runaway cablecar. Is this any kind of life for a diplomat? Is this the reward of a straight-A student at Harvard?

Ah, Harvard. Why had he permitted his hubris about a government career to take him away from the tranquil, ivy-covered walls where he could have enjoyed the sedate existence of a professor on lifetime tenure? There was his class seated before him, their eyes and ears set to drink in his unparalleled genius. "Gentlemen, today I shall lecture upon the use of one hundred-megaton bombs in a limited nuclear war. As a corollary theme I shall discuss how pleasant life could be for the last six people on earth." Halfway through his dissertation all he could read upon the faces of this crewcutted, brown-and-white saddled bunch was a desire to buy a tweed sportcoat from J. Press, pile into a convertible and violate a Vassar girl, and so he had quit the groves of Cambridge for the marble of Washington.

At Lombard Street Dr. Kissingherr's life, which had tried to pass before him some blocks back, gave it another try, but again the images of his youth could not keep up with the even faster rolling car and in disgust the life cried out, "Henry, the hell with it. I can't keep up. You're on your own." And so it would not be a total loss, the life grabbed a passing drunk and began to unfold and soon Henry Kissingherr's history was being screened for a total stranger, who quickly nodded off in boredom.

On bolted the cablecar, like some enraged bull released from the pens of the Plaza de Toros, the frightened Dr. Kissingherr crouching, not knowing what the end would be, where the fatal crash would occur. But scholar that he was, a man who did not believe in wasting the precious moments granted by life, he took out a Flair pen and a yellow pad from the briefcase and sketched out in a few bold strokes the items for a workable settlement of the Middle East crisis. At least in his shattered remains he would leave some kind of brilliant legacy.

At Chestnut Street the cablecar caught a brand-new Chevrolet Vega broadside, smashed into it resoundingly and sent it, now crushed into a whorl of metal, spinning end-over-end until it came to rest on the front lawn of the San Francisco Art Institute which at that moment was holding a competition for sculpture. One look at the crunched-up Vega was enough to convince the judges it was the hands-down winner. They quickly titled it "Transmission Impossible" and sold it to Norton Simon for $58,000, plus tax, license and dealer's prep charges.

Faster, faster, faster careened the cablecar, and now Fisherman's Wharf and the sparkling bay were in clear sight. Screams of "mad cablecar! mad cablecar!" came from the startled throats of restaurant patrons, choking on their cracked crabs and sourdough bread at the sight of the vehicle barreling down on them. They scattered like tenpins, leaving a clear path for the cablecar which now jumped the track and headed full steam toward the fishing boats moving into their landings, filled with their early morning catch.

Then it vaulted high into the air and came crashing down and now the doctor knew he must jump or be squashed when this iron and wood relic disintegrated into splinters. At the last moment he hurled his chubby frame in an ungraceful dive and suddenly he was free of the cablecar which plowed into the water and went down.

He himself flew more than a hundred feet, crashing into something wet and cold. There was the feeling of slime covering his body and he thought, is this death? Is this the end of Dr. Henry Kissingherr?

THIRTEEN

So this was heaven. How different it seemed from all his Biblical notions. No frothy clouds, no rippling of harps, no Throne of Judgment, and to make it even more bizarre all the angels seemed to look like tuna. This is decidedly not a Jewish heaven, he reflected, for there at least the fish would be herring. He felt himself suddenly being yanked upward along with this Neptunian heavenly host and to his amazement he saw he was being borne by a gigantic crane into a cannery.

As he was dropped unceremoniously onto a conveyor belt, he realized that his last-ditch leap from the cablecar had hurled him into the hold of a tuna boat. Now I've gotten to the albacore of the problem, he thought, again manifesting the famed Kissingherr wit, but the humming of the belt indicated a new horror for his still-battered body. If he could not get off in time he would be chewed up with his fellow fishy travelers, packed in oil and canned. And Henry Kissingherr, the dove of peace, would be turned into a Chicken Of The Sea!

He suddenly pushed away his tuna tunic and cried to a young female cannery worker, "Stop immediately! I am Dr. Kissingherr."

"My God," she said. "I have heard of your reputation, but you'll go anywhere to meet a broad, won't you?"

Noticing the fullness of her breasts just yearning for erotic contact, and ascertaining that there was at least another two hundred feet of belt to go before he would end up as a tuna casserole, he told the maiden a fascinating, little-known anecdote about British politician Gladstone. Before he even got to the part about Disraeli she was disrobing, and they had their moment of madness among the popped-out, staring eyes of the tuna. Finally, he bade her a warm farewell and she was soon back separating the losing Charlie the Tunas from the good stuff.

FOURTEEN

Any average citizen looking at the long line bending around Sunset Boulevard into Van Ness Avenue would have thought from the clothes of those in the queue that a state lunatic asylum had been emptied by a flash fire in the laundry room. There was a man dressed in a Ubangi outfit, a loincloth and a bone driven through his nose, not quite in keeping with his blond hair and blue eyes; three white-haired old ladies from Glendale had somehow managed to squeeze into a Siamese twin getup, with ill consequences for the third woman who came out gasping for air every few seconds; an accountant from Altadena had cleverly disguised himself as a huge mutton chop, but bit by bit his camouflage was being stripped away by a ravenous pack of stray dogs. There were others, people dressed as turtles, a husband and wife pen and pencil set (a logical choice: their names were Parker) ; and a usual sprinkling of Frankensteins, Draculas and Wolfmen. Why were all these good citizens so oddly bedecked? Because in a few minutes if luck smiled upon them they would be sitting in the audience of the nation's top giveaway television show, "Let's Squeal for a Deal," starring that affable master of ceremonies, Monte Monte.

And these celebrity-conscious Americans would have shrieked in insane glee if they had known that the short, rotund man at the beginning of the line, dressed as Tarzan, his rubber tire of a belly looping over his leopard briefs, a knife gleaming at his hip, was Dr. Henry Kissingherr.

Why was the presidental superagent in Los Angeles and dressed like the king of the jungle?

The Chinese girl's phrase had haunted him... "Monte Monte"... and at his behest the CIA had quickly identified the popular host. He had taken the obvious course, gone to the show, said, "I am Dr. Kissingherr and I wish to speak to Monte Monte," and had been greeted by a pimply usher's nasty comeback, "No shit, and I'm Donny Osmond. I'm working here because my older brothers won't cut me in on the bread," and had been bounced in an undignified manner. Hence the suit and the need to emit the famed Tarzan yell, which somehow was coming out like a Bavarian yodel. And, he thought, one more self-administered punch to the chest and I shall give myself intercostal neuritis.

His plan was utter simplicity. He would gain entrance to the studio, perhaps even get on the show and find a way to isolate Monte Monte from his staff and question him. At noon the usher poked his head around the door and called, "Come in, legions of greed!" as he scurried out of the path of the pounding hordes.

Dr. Kissingherr found himself, as he had hoped, in the front row, wedged in between a man dressed as a chimpanzee and a chimpanzee dressed as a man, with no discernible difference in personal hygiene, the doctor's nose told him. Out onto the stage bounced a cheery little man in a yachting blazer, ascot and grey slacks. "Hi! I'm Ollie Olson and I'm here to warm you folks up until Monte Monte gets here. Here's a great ice-breaking joke. I knew a man who was so crosseyed that every time he cried the tears ran down his shoulders."

The audience howled at this typical display of Ollie Olson's dynamic wit.

"Now here's how we play 'Let's Squeal for a Deal'," the peppery little warmup man continued. "If we choose you as a contestant and you win you get an all-expenses-paid weekend with a beautiful stewardess from the airline of your choice in Acapulco, with an added bonus—the chaperone is crippled and blind. Oh, my God," he said, an embarrassed flush crawling over his chipmunk cheeks. "That's the prize for 'The Dating Game.' I do so many of these shows I sometimes forget where I am. Okay, let's try again. The rules are these. If you're chosen you'll be offered a choice of cash, that ol' green stuff. Or you can take a chance and go for what's behind Doors One, Two or Three. And you never know what's behind there. Yesterday, we had a lady who got a thousand smackers and chose instead to trade for what was behind Door Two. Alas, all she got was a colony of vicious Brazilian army ants, but it wasn't a total loss. With good old Yankee ingenuity she smeared honey on her body and in no time at all lost fifty-eight ugly pounds. On the other hand we had a man who swapped three dollars for the right to walk through Door Three and he won the biggie... four tons of tapioca, a complete Packard Bell home entertainment unit which includes AM-FM radio, color television, stereo phonograph, cassettes, videotape recordings, plus the fishing rights to all waters within two hundred miles of Uruguay."

Then screams erupted like mini-volcanoes all over the studio as the tanned, smiling Monte Monte himself trode airily into view.

"Monte! Monte! Pick me!... pick me!" And people were falling over each other in a bid to kiss his ring. "Monte! Monte!"

He raised his hand, and a dead silence came over the drooling visages. "Okay, Ollie. Hi, everybody..."

"Monte! Monte!" they screamed anew.

"Are we gonna have fun today, gang?"

"Yeah, yeah, yeah!"the gang yelled back, and just as they stopped he heard a *"Ja"* in the yeahs. It came from the mouth of a chubby man in horn-rimmed glasses squeezed into jungle skivvies.

"Ja?" Monte Monte chuckled. "How do you like that, gang?" We got Martin Bormann in a Tarzan suit. You're on the show, buddy," he laughed, giving Dr. Kissingherr a pat on his curly brown locks.

In a booth above the audience a television director previously in a state of lassitude from taping hundreds of these festivals of greed, snapped out of it with a whiplash-like jerk. God, it couldn't be! That kraut in the jungle suit. It couldn't be! Rafer had put the hit on him in Frisco. It had to be coincidence. But that fleshy nose, that double chin, those horn-rimmed glasses, that paunch, those gnawed fingernails. He put a camera on "Tarzan" and bent forward, an intent expression on his face. And the game began.

Mr. and Mrs. Parker, chosen because "I don't want to break up a set," joshed Monte, were first to try. They were handed a crisp hundred-dollar bill. "There's old Ulysses Grant himself smilin' up at you from his bed of green. Wanna keep him, or go for one of the doors?"

"Go, go, go!" the audience screamed. Mr. Parker, a sixty-dollar-a-week vegetable washer in the produce department of a supermarket, gulped, for he hadn't seen this much cash money since his mustering out pay from the Coast Guard. He attempted to stuff the bill into his pocket and call it a good day's work, but his missus stayed him. "No, Oscar, 'Let's Squeal for a Deal'!"

"Okay," Monte Monte said. "What door?"

"Two," said Mrs. Parker in a tremulous voice. There was a harp glissando and Monte Monte led the Parkers by the hand through its portal.

The crowd groaned, the Parkers' faces fell. There behind Door Two seated on a pile of his own droppings was a fat brown and white pig. "This porker is worth fifty bucks, Mr. and Mrs.

Parker. Or this parker is worth fifty bucks, Mr. and Mrs. Porker," said Monte Monte, who, when the door to top-grade comedy was left ajar, never hesitated to barge in with an ad lib beauty. The husband went glum. He had lost not only fifty dollars but gained twenty pounds of desperately unneeded manure.

"But," said Monte, his eyes atwinkle, "you couldn't very well keep this pig without a pigpen, and where would you find a pigpen? I'll tell you where... on your very own pigfarm!" The crowd began to scream; Mrs. Parker started jumping up and down, spraying blue black ink on the Ubangi man, the Siamese twins and a few other unfortunates. "In Secaucus, New Jersey, one hundred acres valued at $500,000... and to make sure you get a good tax break on your farm, here is your very own United States Congressman..." A distinguished silver-haired solon stepped from behind the pig as Monte Monte continued, "Walker Gordon, a Democrat, who will see to it that for a trifling campaign contribution your taxes will be held to a bare minimum."

"Oh, Marthy," said Mr. Parker. "We're rich... we're rich!" And this little man, who had spent his entire life grubbing out a few hard-earned dollars to keep the Parkers in a bungalow in Gardena, began to jump up and down like a pogo stick gone mad. Then he suddenly clutched at his heart, doubled over and fell face down on the stage. A quick check by the show's attending physician, kept on retainer for these rather frequent occurrences, determined that Mr. Parker would never set foot on his new farm. Under it— but not on.

"We're awfully sorry about that, Mrs. Parker," Monte Monte said, "but you do have the pig, the farm, the money and..."

"Me. I love you, Mrs. Parker," Congressman Gordon said opportunistically. "Will you marry me?" She agreed, Monte Monte, an ordained clergyman, performed the ceremony on stage and the event moved on. And thus it was easy to see why this program had perennially tabbed a fantastic share of the television audience for within the time frame of a few seconds the viewers had seen a rags-to-riches story, a sudden death, sweet, young new love, a marriage... all the elements of life.

"Well, let's get Tarzan up here," Monte Monte cackled. "Boy, you're the chubbiest Tarzan I've ever seen. I guess you keep breaking the vine. Well, Tarz, how's everything in the Belgian Congo?"

Unwittingly, Dr. Kissingherr stopped pounding his chest, dropped his Tarzan yell and responded with crispness: "The situation in the Belgian Congo, once highly volatile in the wake of the ouster of the colonialists and the murder of Lumumba, has begun to stabilize. The tribal wars have diminished, new industries and technologies are in full sway and one may optimistically look forward to an era of concord and harmony."

Television director Greg Fort's sweat was rolling torrentially down his drawn face. That clinched it. The man he held in view on camera four was without a doubt Henry Kissingherr, for in his earphones he could hear the unstoppable analysis of all of Africa's problems rolling on... Kenya, Uganda, Rhodesia, Swaziland. The jaw of Monte Monte dropped in amazement. Fort motioned for an assistant director to keep the show moving and left the control booth, ran into an adjoining room and dialed a long-distance number. "It's him, dammit, it's him!" Fort listened to the quickly given instructions, then broke in. "I think I know how to handle it." He clicked off.

On stage, Monte Monte was now beginning to yawn, for this unusual Germanic type was now discussing the root causes of the enmity between the Masai and the KiKuyu and, interesting though it might be, one more minute of this and audiences all over the country would either nod off to sleep or use their remote control channel changers to switch over to "Return to Peyton Place."

"That's very intriguing, Tarzan. I'm sure you and Jane must have some exciting conversations in the treehouse. Tell you what, I'll skip the cash part and let you pick any door you want."

"Will it be possible to see you after the show on a personal matter, Herr Monte Monte?" Tarzan asked.

"Oh, sure, sure," the host said. "Now... the door."

"I shall select Door Number Three."

Monte Monte waved his hand. "Go ahead, and good luck."

In the booth Greg Fort tensed. He saw the bulky ape-man turn the knob and at that exact moment the director pulled a lever. Henry Kissingherr stepped over the threshold and, in an instant, *disappeared!* Monte Monte recoiled in horror. "Stop the tape!" he cried. "Well, folks, we're having a slight technical problem, but Ollie will tell you a few jokes while we're fixing things up. We'll find old Tarz, don't you worry."

The little warmup man hustled to center stage. "Did you hear the one about the drunk and the parking meter? He stuck a coin in, saw the arrow move to the number sixty and said, 'Cheez, I just lost a hundred pounds!' "

But the gales of laughter were not heard by Henry Kissingherr, now sliding at breakneck speed down a galvanized iron chute to only heaven knew where!

FIFTEEN

Like a child popping out of a womb, the almost naked Dr. Kissingherr shot out of the uterine tunnel he had been sliding through, to land headfirst against a packing crate. A flash of pain seared his head, but he shook it off and climbed to his feet.

He was in what seemed to be a kind of giant warehouse or stockroom, composed of rows upon rows of crates. On one side he could see shiny new automobiles, refrigerators, television sets, dining room suites, and from another part of the vast room he heard the lowing noise of what he assumed to be an animal of some sort.

And then he saw something that sent a tremor through his brush-burned body.

The muzzle of a gun in the hand of a fortyish, tall, muscular man with a handlebar moustache, a thick head of hair and a maroon velvet jumpsuit whose knees and elbows featured the currently popular patches of daisies, butterflies and likenesses of Barbra Streisand.

"You are probably wondering where you are, Herr Kissingherr," the man said.

"There has been some mistake. I am not Herr Kissingherr. I am Tarzan, is it not so?" He gave his chest another few punches, then winced.

"Ach, it appears I have aggravated my sternum. But please put away the weapon. Let us negotiate whatever small points of difference exist between us. Who are you, sir?"

"Greg Fort, director of this show, and you have landed in the 'Let's Squeal for a Deal' warehouse under the studio where we store all the prizes donated by various manufacturers. You got here so abruptly because this studio was converted from an old burlesque theater. This room is where props were kept, and the trap door into which you fell was used for comedy disappearing acts, as in the famous old burlesque sketch, 'The Wife, The Husband and the Plumber.' Many a baggy-pants Dutch comic came flying through that door, yelling 'cheese n' crackers'! If this room could talk, you'd hear the sounds of old-time burlesque routines, the twanging of G-strings and third-rate comics trying to molest second-rate strippers and winding up with fourth-stage paresis. Yes, in this very room that old warhorse of the midway, Gypsy Sally and her disappearing dove, practiced her act. Where the dove disappeared was known only by Gypsy Sally and her gynecologist. And in this room, crowded with creaky memories of old show biz, you, Henry Kissingherr, will die."

"Why are you threatening my life, Mr. Fort? Since you obviously know who I am and why I am here, what is your role in this affair and, more importantly, where is my leader?"

"My dear Herr Doktor," Fort said, keeping that gun trained on the belly, "I, Greg Fort, am one of the most abused persons ever to man a camera in this industry. I started out on the old 'Cissy Doody' puppet show on the Dumont Network in New York during television's infancy. My brilliant camera work and direction made that little wooden bastard look good to the point where he was pulling in five grand a week. And when Cissy Doody went on national television did he take me along for the ride? Like hell he did. I was fired. Imagine me, Greg Fort, fired by a puppet! That mahogany mothergrabber! I hope to God he has terminal termites."

"A tough break, indeed," the doctor noted.

"Wait, there's more," and now on Fort's face a whole picture of past indignities and insults was being screened—in Accutron, of course. "But I hung in and I went to the networks with a brand new concept for a quiz show, 'The Thirty-Two Thousand Dollar Question'; they laughed, said it couldn't be done, then someone came up with 'The Sixty-Four Thousand Dollar Question,' which they bought because they said it was twice as good as mine, it ran for years and they got rich, but ol' Greg got the shaft again."

In his anger his teeth clenched and a pair of thousand-dollar caps crumbled to chalk. He continued, "Finally, I created the concept of 'Let's Squeal for a Deal' and they loved it, but not with me as the host as I had planned, emerging from anonymity behind the camera to the stardom and adulation I so richly deserve. No, they brought in this Canadian carpetbagger, this mountie named Monte, and he gets the big bread, the screams, the chicks, and I—Greg Fort, who made it all happen—just push the buttons and take my weekly salary, which is more than adequate, but money isn't everything. But I will be the star of this show, I will be, as soon as this country is taken over by... He bit his lip, halted his tirade. "I've told you too much."

"Then Monte Monte has no connection with this monstrous scheme."

"Nah," Fort grunted. "I probably mentioned his name a little too loudly at Ronrico, and somebody talked. Maybe that Chinese broad. But she won't blab any more and neither will you."

Now Greg Fort moved in and in doing so kicked a round object which came skittering across the cement toward the prisoner. "A soccer ball," he chuckled, "one of the prizes donated by the Wilson Sporting Goods Company."

But Henry Kissingherr, seeing the soccer ball, was taken out of the warehouse by his mind and transported back in time to the soft greensward of an athletic field in Fertz, Bavaria, where he stood as a young boy in short striped pants, a jersey, and high stockings. There was Momma beseeching him, "Heinz, please don't play today. Those vicious little Nazi boys are just spoiling for a fight."

And indeed, on the sidelines were wolf packs of the fair-haired, sullen-eyed Hitler Youth, the same bullies who beat him up almost daily on his way to the all-Jewish school he had been forced to attend, and they were screaming like robots, "Juden! Juden!" (Jews! Jews!) But so fanatical a soccer fan was young Heinz that he played that day for Dr. Herzl Zion Hebrew School against Heinrich Himmler Prep, being kicked more times than the ball and once during a particularly brutal drive being kicked into the net, thus becoming the Nazis' winning goal. Now his old hatred returned and on the ball he could see the face of a jeering young Brownshirt and suddenly his leg was lashing out at it with the power of a Pele and on a brown blur it flew, smashing the hand of Fort, sending the gun flying over the floor.

Dr. Kissingherr chugged down an aisle with amazing speed for one so bulbous; what he lacked in agility he more than made up for in panic. He crouched behind a row of crates, shuddering because the maddened Fort had retrieved his gun and was firing, the bullets ricocheting off Westinghouse freezers and Ford Torinos.

Fort was blasting anything that moved. A bullet whacked into flesh and the terrorized doctor saw a gentle, brown-eyed Guernsey cow, obviously a contest gift, gasp her last moo and slump to the ground in a mass of udders, hoofs and legs. The tail gave a final swish and he knew that poor Bossy had gone to a cow's heaven—Green Pastures.

When he heard the clumping steps and Fort's stream of curses, and saw the gun again poke around a corner, he knew it was time for a desperate ploy. He hurled the full weight of his body into a row of cartons which tipped over and caused a cascading of objects of all kinds throughout the warehouse. An enormous pile crashed down on Fort, there was a scream, the splintering of glass, and then quiet.

Greg Fort, indeed, had his face on television as he had so dearly wished. It had been rammed clear through the screen of a twenty-five-inch console model, whose picture tube had severed his jugular vein. Before he had reached the Zenith of his career and become the Admiral of his own show, Magnavox had done him in.

Looking down at his dead foe, Henry Kissingherr felt a queasiness. It was one thing to head up a 151-member staff dedicated to working out scenarios that might wipe out all civilization in a hydrogen war—that was abstract. It was another thing to actually end a man's life, no matter how just the battle, as he had just done. Giving a final nod of sadness to poor deranged Greg Fort, the diplomat took hold of the dead cow's tail, slung it over his shoulder and inch by inch dragged the creature toward an exit sign.

Why not? he thought. With the catastrophic cost of meat caused by his own administration, sad to say, a man had to grab a steak wherever he found one.

SIXTEEN

"Four score and seven years ago," Lincoln said to the wind, "our forefathers..."

"Why are you doing that old number?" Jefferson asked the Great Emancipator.

"I'll say anything to keep from going mad from that incessant clanging on the cliff. He's at it again."

"Bouillon! Bouillon! Bouillon!" cried Teddy Roosevelt.

"Heavens to Betsy Ross," said Washington. "The noise has even gotten to our twentieth century colleague. He's forgetting his 'bully!' shtick, too."

But the man dangling from the rope went on from deepest night until the dawn's early light, banging, cackling and crying out, "Soon, soon, soon..."

SEVENTEEN

On the commercial jet back to Washington, Dr. Henry Kissingherr sat in a miasma of rock-bottom gloom, scarcely noticing that all the stewardesses had recognized him and were undressing as rapidly as they could. He did snap out of it long enough to autograph a few pantyhosed behinds, but as for anything more emotional, it was out of the question. How could a man think of love who had just killed? Why, why, he raged inwardly, could he not have been lucky enough to push a twelve-inch Sony down on Fort and just maim him? Keep him alive? Pump him for more needed data to smash this plot?

He munched insouciantly on the usual first-class airline dinner, opening with a tureen of mock turtleneck sweater soup, baked Cornish Rock Hen (in economy they were only getting the rock, no hen), and a heady but not overpowering magnum of eighty-six-proof Johnson's Glo-Coat, latest of the pop wines.

At Dulles International he was met by the heads of CIA and FBI, who, when they saw his own grim countenance, knew he had not achieved results. There was some attempt at lighthearted talk to relieve the onus all in the speeding limousine were feeling. FBI told a little known story about the ambush of John Dillinger outside the Biograph Theater in Chicago, who, as he lay in that stinking alley with forty-eight G-man slugs in him, said, "This is definitely a case of police brutality." CIA, not to be outdone, told some amusing yarns about the fun side of the heroin trade, but underneath, all felt a growing sense of panic. This was underscored when CIA plucked a document out of his briefcase and handed it to the doctor. "This is a memo from the Russian ambassador to his number one. Unknown to them we cracked their cipher."

The doctor adjusted his horn-rims and read: "Honorable Chairman: I have news of the gravest sort. Yesterday, after much urging, the President of the United States agreed to give me an audience at Camp David on a certain matter well-known to you. Our meeting started off pleasantly enough, but then something extraordinary occurred. He began to do what Americans call a stand-up comedy act, featuring some of the worst jokes I have ever heard. When I did not laugh he said in panic, 'Are you sure you're the regular Russian ambassador?' Then he switched into impressions of film actors Jimmy Stewart, Kirk Douglas, Burt Lancaster and Oliver Hardy. He then tried to sell me six comedy LPs and a table for twenty at the Latin Casino nightclub in Cherry Hill, New Jersey. Old comrade, I fear I was talking to an impostor, however closely he resembled the chief executive in looks and voice. It is my belief that something terrible has happened to the genuine president, a coup d'etat, an illness, etc. If this is true, we may have to go on full nuclear alert immediately."

The doctor sighed. "Have they?"

CIA said, "Our satellites have spotted missiles in place, Red subs on the move and inside info from Russia says all military leaves have been canceled. Naturally, the Pentagon has ordered the same kind of alert. Somehow even Monaco found out and they loaded their flintlock. And while the world goes about its business, hoping PEPPER will save it, there's an Armageddon in the making."

In Operation Quaker Snatchback the computer boys had run a profile check on Fort. Indeed, his television history had rung true; it was also noted that he was a member of several charitable organizations, among them the Mothers March on Colic, the Reindeers March on Hoof and Mouth Disease, and television coordinator for the recent, unsuccessful primary campaign of Senator Humbert Homefree, the Democrat from the wheat-growing midwestern state of Ceresota.

A fast phone call to the Ceresotan was in order, and the doctor caught him during a recess at the Senate Chamber from a heated debate on capital punishment. The Senator's oft-stated position was that a man should not be executed twice for the same crime—"that's double jeopardy"—but should be executed only once, and then serve no more than seven to ten for any subsequent murders.

"Well, I'm pleased as punch to hear from you, Hank," the perky senator said. "But where in the heck is that boss of yours? Golly, we've been trying to huddle with him on a couple of important issues, but he's just not available. I don't mind if a man keeps a low profile, but your guy is making the Invisible Man stick out like a sore thumb."

"I'm sure he will be meeting with you shortly, but in the meantime, I would like to make a discreet inquiry about a former aide of yours, Herr Greg Fort."

"Crazy ol' Greg? What's he done?"

"Oh, his name came up during a conversation about a possible FCC position. Is there anything you can tell me about him?"

"Competent feller, but a trifle nutty. You know those show biz types. Always thinking somebody was out to give him a hosing. Real paranoid. I finally had to fire him when we went to a Los Angeles Dodgers game. The manager and the catcher went to the mound to talk to the pitcher and ol' Greg thought they were plotting against him. Well, Hank," the senator said. "Gotta go back to the floor. The roll call is just about to come up." So that was that for Fort, a nut with an axe to grind, an easy prey for some grand designer, but apparently his secret had died with him. But he had lived long enough to furnish one significant piece of information. Whoever had the president was not just trying to keep him from the PEPPER talks; he was trying to take over the country itself. But now the seconds kept ticking away... the Congress of Vienna was drawing nearer... and all he had accomplished was to brush against the lives of a Chinese sex kitten, an evil acupuncturist, a pornographer and a television director. Two of them were dead, and he was no nearer to the solution.

As he sat in his chair at the head of the operational table, the secretary of state came in beaming from ear to ear. "No luck in L.A., eh, Henry? Well, I understand even Einstein messed up now and then trying to add up a dinner check. Boy, I'm sure glad I don't have the knowledge that if I fail it's World War III. Have a good night, Henry. I'm going out in the hallway and deface your portrait."

A clear sign of malevolence, the harried doctor thought. This man is not with me.

EIGHTEEN

At 5 A.M. old Chanticleer, the commune's rooster, did not even make it up to the fencepost to crow his wake-up call and, frankly, didn't give a damn. He was zonked out because another fun-loving commune dweller had dropped a little Acapulco Gold in his mash so he had sent a mynah bird to do the job. And the mynah, not equipped with the vocal power of the rooster, lisped a feeble "Hi, guys... rise and shine" and the commune again greeted the dawn.

In the masked man's lodge the drugged president lay sleeping on a bed of straw. The conservative elements who had elected him would have been shocked to see the defender of the old values clad in Levi's, an Indian headband and a T-shirt that said, "Keep on truckin'."

Now they let him sleep alongside the vice president, dressed in blue jeans, his own T-shirt with the face of Wonder Wart Hog on it, because the last injection had finally broken through the layers of mental resistance. After a stream of hidden fantasies which included an urge to go into an Orange County voting booth and pull the Democratic lever, they had struck gold. Out rolled the complete U.S. stance for the PEPPER talks, the carefully documented positions, the bargaining leverage... it was all there.

"Congratulations, Dr. Street," and the masked man gave the physician's hand a vigorous pump. "Now I have a clear path to power, with just one little overweight, rotund roadblock in horn-rimmed glasses and drip-dry suit. He must be eliminated. He is the one man who even at this late date could step in and take over at Vienna, the one man with the acumen to discover us. He has already come too close on several occasions. But he has an Achilles heel, in his case located in his groin. He can not resist conquering a beautiful woman and that is just the sort we shall send him."

NINETEEN

Somehow his eyes were still clear, but now a red rim of fatigue had formed around the ridges of his glasses. Yet Dr. Kissingherr pushed on, collating, probing, examining again and again in his mind the events he had undergone, sifting them for a possible clue.

An aide tapped his shoulder timidly. "Dr. Kissingherr, a long distance call from New York City."

"Is it a paid call?" the ever frugal doctor inquired.

"Yes. It's a woman who says she knows you. Glory Steinway."

For the first time in many pressure-packed hours the doctor smiled. Glory Steinway, the ultramilitant spokeswoman for the women's lib movement, the bra burner, the editor of *Mizz Magazine,* whose monthly centerfold usually featured a male being forced into unnatural acts, such as scrubbing floors and changing diapers, usually at the mercy of a woman wielding a cat o' nine tails. Glory Steinway, who had held him up to scorn in her columns and speeches as the prototypical male chauvinist pig. Indeed, his mind wandered back to a congressional dinner where he had stated the nationally quoted witticism, "Glory Steinway is not now and has never been my girl friend. But I am not discouraged. After all, she did not say that if nominated she would not accept or if elected she would not serve." This had provoked howls of laughter from the other male chauvinist pigs.

Why was this leggy, quick-witted filly, who had popularized throughout New York the Steinway look, granny glasses and long flowing blonde hair, a look so distinctive that even some women were emulating it, why was she calling him now?

"Henry?" The voice was silvery, seductive.

"Ja, Fraulein... Miss... Mizz... whatever you are at the moment."

"Tonight it's Glory to you," the voice throbbed.

Glory Hallelujah, he mentally enthused. "How charming to hear from you. What may I do for you?"

"Henry, I'm having a little party at the magazine tonight. I'd adore having you. You're the only attractive man I could think of wanting to be near. Just an intimate party. Lennie will perform his new Mass for Twelve-Toned Triangle... Truman will read a few passages from his latest book, *Son of Cold Blood...* Polly is going to do an interpretive dance in Turtle Oil... John and Yoko, Yoko and Ono, Ono and Yes-Yes, Yes-Yes and Zsa-Zsa... just everyone whose ass is worth kissing will be there."

"I am truly overwhelmed, Glory," he replied, "especially in view of your past antagonisms, but it appears I am terribly tied up at the moment."

"A shame," she cooed. "There was somebody special who wanted to meet you... Ronrico." With a clink the horn-rims slid from his fleshy nose into an ashtray. Ronrico, the home base for the conspiracy!

Why, out of the blue, would Glory pass the peace pipe and drop that name now of all times? He would jet to New York to find out.

"On second thought, perhaps I can steal away from affairs of state for a few affairs in the city," he said suavely, his Continental humor at razor-sharpness. He took the address of *Mizz Magazine,* heard her whisper, "Goodnight, Henry," and hung up.

TWENTY

The first thing to hit Dr. Kissingherr's senses upon entering the bustling ambience at *Mizz Magazine* was the tinkling piano of Manhattan's favorite interpreter of sophisticated show tunes. The elfin Negro, Bobby Squirt, was playing a few Cole Porter songs so obscure they had been actually written by Irving Berlin. The next was the tinkling of a hundred cocktail glasses, the third the sound of one of the Beautiful People, too drunk to make it to the john, tinkling into an ice bucket.

The VIPs, as Glory had promised, were there in full force. At one end of the room was the inseparable trio, Jackie, resplendent in a floor-length diamond; Ari, on the phone wrapping up a deal to have all his oil tankers painted for $29.95 each by Earl Scheib; and that pestiferous photographer who had made a total career out of taking the lady's picture. Now he had disguised himself as a waiter and his flashbulbs as hors d'oeuvres. Some of the partygoers seemed annoyed by the chopped liver that popped off blindingly in their faces.

Harold Susann and Jacqueline Robbins, the nation's top sex book authors, sat in a corner exchanging literary gossip, techniques, and phone numbers. Millionaire horse fancier Whit Jockney poured a drink for his date for the evening, the exciting, satin-skinned Arabian beauty, Agoura Khan, a 4,000-pound racehorse he had just purchased.

As the celebrants passed into an adjoining reception room they were greeted by a gauntlet of burnoosed Black September terrorists. With drawn guns they collected jewels, furs, and cash; from those who came empty-handed, they accepted BankAmericards. "How radically chic!" one of the Beautiful People gushed. "Last year it was the Panthers. Glory's always up to date."

But all the chattering ceased when Dr. Kissingherr entered. "It's him..." the whispers flew about the party. On the faces of the liberated women, who wore faded blue-denim creations by St. Laurent and faded blue sapphires to match, was a kind of mixed emotion: hatred for all that he as presidential advisor and superstud stood for and yet a sneaking fascination to be held in the embrace of a man who held the world in his embrace.

The latest rage of the cocktail world, tomato juice mixed with Mogen David wine, a Bloody Murray, was pressed into his hand by a waiter. Then all eyes turned to an elevator door which opened to reveal the hostess, Glory Steinway, her sharp, pretty little face framed by those glasses, her brownish hair with sandy streaks and those fantastic thighs outlined by tight-fitting French pants.

The Beautiful People hushed like a jet of water stopped by a twist of the faucet. They waited for the confrontation sure to ensue because of Glory's past acidulous prose in *Mizz Magazine* about the doctor. Surely he had been invited here for sport. Her tart tongue would cut this academic genius to smithereens. But they gasped. She held him about the waist and brushed his cheek with her lips. "Oh, Henry, I'm so glad you could come."

He brought his heels together again in his suave continental manner, this time ramming his ankle bones and thinking, *Gottenu,* I must desist from this practice. I am clicking myself to death. There goes my fifth pair of Thom McAns this month.

Arm in arm, this glittering couple moved about, shaking hands with other guests, sipping their drinks, greeting new arrivals but pausing time and again to flash signals into each other's eyes.

"Henry, why don't you come upstairs to my apartment? We have so much to talk about," she whispered. "We won't be missed."

On the way to the elevator they passed Drs. Atkins and Stillman overeating like mad and being egged on by the tall, blonde lady who headed the famous Weight Watchers organization. "Keep at it, guys," she smiled, and gave them applications for membership.

Up zipped the Otis to Glory's private residence and in its closeness he could catch the scent of her enticing fragrance, "Muskie," the new craze in perfume taken from the glands of a Polish musk deer.

Glory's place was a shambles, but a well-organized one. Books and pamphlets were piled in stacks all over the floor, and he could spot such titles as *Vasectomy: A Brand New Ball Game, The Angela Davis Cookbook, Orgasms For The Masses* by Clitoris Leachman, and similar far-out tracts. On a coffee table was a huge bowl of fashionable granola, the popcorn of the organic set, two tiny figurines depicting Germaine Greer kicking Norman

Mailer in the groin, and a vibrator autographed "To Darling Glory—from the Daughters of Billitis."

"Relax, Henry. I'm going to change into something more comfortable." And she disappeared into the bathroom.

While she changed, he looked out at New York at night, its beribboned avenues of light. Somehow he found his owlish eyes straying to Yorkville, the German section on the East Side to which he and his family had gravitated after their escape from Hitlerism. *Ach,* Yorkville, a hotbed of Bund activities in the late 1930s, swastikas flaunted openly, Nazis speechifying on street corners, Fritz Kuhn the local fuhrer and his bullyboys everpresent. In the Café Goering there were only two classes of people, Nazi spies and FBI waiters, plus Signe Hasso who sat in a corner sipping Liebfraumilch and gathering background material for her role in *The House on Ninety-second Street.*

Here Momma cooked for wealthy German Jews and Poppa worked as a lowly clerk. And here Heinz, who had changed his name to Henry because the Germanic version sounded like a goosestep (Heinz-Tzvai-Drei! Heinz-Tzvai-Drei!), became an all A-student at George Washington High, was drafted into the Army, got a post-war governmental scholorship to Harvard where he was *summa cum laude* in 1950, a Ph.D. in 1954. Then the failed marriage, which had produced the two lovely, ultrabright (in a nondental way) children, his ascent up the ladder of government, his thought-provoking, influential book on atomic warfare, *Nuclear Blasts and Foreign Policy* (which his publisher had given the more marketable title, *The Nuclear Warfare Diet Book*), his role as advisor to New York's governor, a presidential aspirant, dining at Nelson's house on Oysters Rockefeller (oysters wrapped in thousand-dollar bills), then his fateful meeting with the man he had first scornfully rejected as chief executive material but later was to serve with unswerving allegiance.

His nostalgia was shattered in a most delightful way when Glory reentered in nothing but a Saran Wrap caftan revealing the kind of goodies definitely not in the leftover category.

"Ronrico," he breathed, frantically trying to maintain his composure. "Tell me about Ronrico." But now she was letting the caftan slip to the floor and undoing his drip-dry suit. "Ronrico," he said again, in an attempt to further his mission.

But she stilled his queries with a kiss. "Later, Henry, but first..."

Twenty minutes later, after a Steinway had been played as never before, not even by Arthur Rubinstein, the doctor and his love partner lay on her burlap sheets, spent and content.

"Now, Glory, tell me all you know about Ronrico. I understand our political orientations are vastly at variance, but you must know that if this plot succeeds the fate of the world may be in the balance. Do you know about Ronrico? Were you there? Why?"

She lit a cigarette, took a deep hit and unconsciously puffed out the letters "MALE CHAUVINIST PIG." Leaning on her elbow she spoke softly and seriously. "Yes, I was there with the others, Henry. My movement can see no gains for women, for minorities, for any of the downtrodden with your commander in power."

"Tell me more about that conference," he pleaded, but the cool, worldly look was back in Glory's eyes and again granny glasses and horn-rimmed glasses locked bumpers and she led him into a second bout of passion that left him jellyfish weak. And his eyes closed.

Dr. Kissingherr stirred and panted, "Glory, Glory..." He moved his lips, but found them pressing the roughness of burlap, not her soft silky hair. Glory Steinway was gone. He looked on his left wrist at the face of the Phillipe Patique watch of twenty-four-carat gold given to him by the president on whose back was an inscription, "To Henry, who has always made things perfectly clear—RMN," a watch which told the seconds, the minutes, the hours, the day of the month, his horoscope, his weight, the airline schedules to Paris and the hours of operation of a massage parlor in Los Angeles. Four A.M. My God, had he been sleeping all that time? Thanks to Glory's sexual Sominex he had finally been able to relax from the crushing pressure burdening him since the kidnap ensued. But where was she? Her side of the bed was still warm, but she had gone. To the party downstairs? Was it still going on?

He rose to flick on a bedside lamp and when the light blazed, he fell back on the bed with a start. There climbing through the window was a lithe man, bronze of face, his jet-black hair braided, a plum-colored velvet jacket with a colorful scarf, a beaded belt of turquoise holding up midnight blue flare pants and on his feet soundless moccasins.

All this the doctor was to notice later, but the first things he did spot were the fury in the man's black eyes and...

A tomahawk in his hand.

"Oh, Great Spirit, Thou who rulest all tribes and lodges, field and stream, better homes and gardens, make my hand mighty so that I may slay this oppressor of all Indians." He looked upward, invoking his deity, and crying out as he stamped his foot daintily. "Oh, come on, Great Spirit, darling, get it on..."

From the tomahawk-wielder's manner it was clear to Dr. Kissingherr that he faced catastrophe at the hands of an individual representative of two minorities: Indian and Gay Lib. This was made even more clear when he spotted an inscription on the tomahawk that read, "To my darling brave, Running Funny, from your adoring lover, Sitting Tool." And instead of the strong earthy smells of venison and pine trees this individual exuded a commercial cologne, but it did retain something of an Indian feel, for it was Canoe.

Still naked, the doctor climbed out from under the burlap blanket and revealed himself to the Indian, whose hand and its deadly weapon began an ominous rise.

"You must stop this immediately, my friend. I am no oppressor to Indians or gays. My heart is filled with understanding for all people for I too, am a member of a downtrodden minority. I am Jewish."

"I noticed," said Running Funny, a sudden constriction in his throat.

"Whatever your grievances are against society, surely we can settle them by negotiations."

But that seemed to infuriate Running Funny. "Always negotiations. Always broken treaties. White man speak with forked tongue." And that last phrase seemed to cause a delicious shiver. He let out a war whoop, but as he looked upon the doctor's unclothed body there was very little war in that whoop. "Oh," he said with some regret, "what a waste. But your time is at hand. My tribe of gay Indians, better known as the Sweet Sioux, has marked you for death and thanks to Glory it'll be a three-Lib hit." But despite his murderous errand, his eyes continued to sweep the doctor's frame.

The doctor perceived the obvious interest and knew what he must do. In order to save myself for America, I must be up for it, he thought. To think that the future of the land of the free must hinge on my ability to stand tall for my country. He closed his eyes tightly, let that awesome gray matter in his mind begin to exercise its full power. Think, think of erotic images that will cause an erection, he pleaded to that mega-brain. And the images began to flicker across his mind like the leader strip of a film... four, three, two, one...

The first ones were resounding failures... the shape of the peace table in Paris (nothing erotic there, he thought), a samovar in the hands of Kosygin pouring him a glass of tea (nothing there, either)... and the face of the vice president railing against the "effete snobs" (definitely nothing there). Think, think *hot,* he begged his brain, for the tomahawk was now beginning to descend and then he hit gold, the golden fuzzy triangle of a secretary in the Pentagon, the breasts of a lady columnist from the *Washington Post,* the alabaster buttocks of Trudi Brown, a starlet who had used him while he was using her... and the images were flashing like a montage of makeouts... thighs, mammaries, calves... and then it happened.

Dr. Henry Kissingherr rose in a color carousel of red, white and blue... perhaps not the flag, but certainly the flagpole.

With a gasp Running Funny dropped his tomahawk, his passion driving the murder from the dark eyes, the Gay driving the Indian off the reservation of his heart...

He lunged at the diplomat who swiveled adroitly causing the Sioux to miss the mark and ram headlong into a pile of Glory's books.

The doctor backed fearfully away, his hindquarters coming in contact with the windowsill through which the Indian had climbed. The cool dawn air shivered his timbers, but now Running Funny spun, charged again with mad lust. He leaped out at his part's desire, but the doctor ducked, and through the window flew Running Funny to his doom, twenty stories below. There was a trailing scream. He had fallen on a confederate waiting in the street, another Indian, coincidentally named Trailing Scream.

"*Auf wiedersehn* and *shalom,* Running Funny," whispered the doctor to the crushed body on the cement. "As they say in South Dakota, that's the way the Sioux Falls."

Donning his drip-dry and tie, the presidential advisor took the elevator to the street and walked out into the bustling New York morning, again having escaped death, no nearer to the solution, the PEPPER talks a day closer, and with a score to settle with Glory Steinway.

TWENTY-ONE

I t was 8:15 A.M. when he checked into his suite at the Waldorf, the lines of stress ever deepening on his pudgy cheeks. He glanced through the messages sent from Operation Quaker Snatchback, all reflecting gloom and uncertainty.

The CIA boss walked in as he was examining the Eyes Only cables. "Henry, any luck yet? They're setting up for the Congress of Vienna and there's no doubt that the others will be there for the sake of appearance, but we know damn well they've got their fingers on the trigger and so have we. If the president doesn't attend the opening plenary session in two days we may have to tell the country, follow the laws of presidential succession and, God, won't that raise the dust! Internal panic, external holocaust, who knows?"

"I feel I am on to something," and he recounted the Glory Steinway episode.

"Then we'll pick her up immediately and question her on this Ronrico business," said CIA.

"No, I would prefer that she be allowed to roam free. She doubtless believes I am dead. I shall personally shadow Miss Steinway until she leads me to the head of this conspiracy. Give me two more days and I shall have the president and vice president at the Congress of Vienna, I swear it."

To relieve the tension they ordered breakfast, and while munching on sweet rolls and sipping Sanka, the doctor turned on the popular "Good Morning Show" with host Barbara Voltaire. Newsman Frank Magoo was running over the headlines, the lead item, of course, the seclusion of the president and speculation surrounding it. Other items included the terms of a ceasefire worked out between William Buckley and Gore Vidal, and Ralph Nader announcing that he had been successful in not only recalling 45,000 defective automobiles but a like number of defective St. Christopher statuettes on their dashboards. Then the show went into its usual round of guest celebrities. Magoo interviewed the producer of the notorious film, *Deep Throat*, who revealed that the budget for this big-grossing film had been a mere pittance, $20,000 for the production and $50,000 for lozenges. "Wild Cherry was her favorite," the filmmaker revealed.

Then critic Gene Screwit, he of the Brillo Afro, the walrus moustache and the caustic eye, did his five minutes, ripping to pieces six new movies, four Broadway musicals and a twelve-car collision on the Long Island Expressway, commenting on the latter, "It lacked drama. They do these things better on the Belt Parkway."

The doctor was changing his shirt, the CIA chief so shaken by the events of the last few days that he took off his clean shirt and put on the doctor's old one, when both froze at the conclusion of the Alpo commercial showing Ed MacMahon being bitten by a cocker spaniel. There sitting next to Barbara Voltaire, that cool smile on her sharp face, those long legs crossed, was Glory Steinway.

"The talk is, Glory, that you and Dr. Kissingherr were very chummy at a *Mizz Magazine* bash last night," Barbara said cattily.

"Nonsense. I just invited that heel-clicking Teuton over to let the air out of him. He didn't even get a hearty handshake at the door, much less whatever he's supposed to be famous for. With this mizz he mizzed, believe me."

Barbara chuckled at the Steinway riposte.

"But that's not why I'm here this morning, Barbara," Glory said, stubbing out her cigarette in Frank Magoo's palm, another manifestation of her disdain for male chauvinist pigs. "I want all women who feel that sense of oppression to join me today in a gigantic rally at Central Park at noon. Come, my sisters, come by the thousands 'cause we're gonna tell it like it is." She gave a clenched fist salute which somehow ended up on the jaw of a cameraman and by the time she had left there was a trail, stretching from the set to the studio door, of fifteen men, wincing, holding their battered faces and karate-kicked legs, some totally unconscious.

And Henry Kissingherr knew where the next leg of his odyssey would be, Manhattan's playground of the poor, Central Park.

TWENTY-TWO

T he Sheep Meadow was already thronged by thousands of women of all shades and sizes, moving toward the hastily constructed platform upon which sat Glory Steinway and her coleaders of the movement. And more were pouring in from all sides of the park, disgorged by cabs, buses, and anything else that moved. Quite a few had come to the rally on the backs of their husbands, flicking whips and calling out, "Faster, Seymour, faster!" or "Mush, Marty, mush!"

There was a contingent of radical nuns, holding banners, "WHY CAN'T A WOMAN BE POPE?"

"LET US HERE CONFESSIONS ONCE IN A WHILE. WHY SHOULD ONLY THE PRIESTS HERE THE GOOD STUFF?" Next to them were some Catholic laywomen (who despised that term for obvious reasons) calling out their own slogans, "The Church wouldn't be anti-pill if the Pope was a Pop!" Some of the ladies were sneering openly at the mounted police trying to keep order. "Why can't we be brutalized by *female* mounted police?", they stormed at New York's finest. A Lesbian contingent, there to protest the oppression practiced against their kind, found themselves pressed up against some of the others and forgot their stated reasons for being there. They began to cop a few feels and make assignations. The ranks kept swelling... matrons from Westchester rubbed shoulders with tiny Puerto Rican garment workers, telephone operators rubbed shoulders with haughty saleswomen from Bonwits and Saks, and the ever-opportunistic Lesbians were rubbing shoulders with everybody.

On the edge of the crowd Dr. Kissingherr trained his field glasses on Glory Steinway's body, smiled at the recollection of those curvy flanks he had outflanked the night before, and moved closer to the platform.

On the stand now was Bella Fireplug, the squat, peppy congresswoman, first firing broadsides at male dominance; as she warmed up she began to verbally assault racism, poverty, the boredom of the auto assembly line, municipal corruption, poor housing, lackluster education. She concluded with a tirade at The Maker for causing typhoons, earthquakes, and excessive humidity. Next was Betty Freed'em, one of the movement's founders. In a low-key but nonetheless powerful speech she implored men to understand a woman's needs, to empathize in every way, and if possible, to bear children. Both received prolonged applause, and then the fiery acknowledged Lesbian, Kate Mallet, hammered away at the inequities of the man-woman relationship to more thunderous applause.

There was a ceremonial burning of the effigies of all symbols of male chauvinism... straw figures with cartoon faces depicting Hugh Hefner (his effigy was torched by Glory flinging a flaming Bunny tail onto it)... James Bond... Burt Reynolds... Joe Namath (they set fire to his full-length black mink). Finally Glory, mike in hand, stilled the shrieking crowd. "And here," she snarled, pointing at the last unburned effigy, "is the so-called superstud of the diplomatic world, a man whose legendary conquests of women have furthered the myths of women as toys of the boudoir. You all know the face of this sexual facist... this Powerkraut."

Then she blinked. For there in the crowd she had spotted the real face of Dr. Henry Kissingherr. My Goodness, he's here! They told me he was to be kidnapped but how in the name of Medea did he get away? That damn, damn Teuton!

"My fellow women, you will be shocked to learn that this man is actually among us now, jeering at everything we stand for. There he is... Dr. Henry Kissingherr!"

When an angry murmur, like millions of disturbed hornets rose from the packed crowd of womanhood, she quaked, for now they had spotted him and were moving ominously toward the diplomat, eyes red with fury, Revlon nails set to rake him into shreds. "Kill Kissingherr!" a loud voice commanded, and soon the cry was taken up by all. "Kill Kissingherr... kill... kill..."

"No, no! I didn't mean," but Glory's voice was drowned out by the bloodthirsty din and she realized this would be as impossible to stop as a crowd of women trying to break into Klein's for a Washington's Birthday sale.

The terrorized Dr. Kissingherr, now panting as he dashed through the inflamed masses, running for his very life, was dodging a hatpin thrust by an irate grandmother, a purse swung by an irate hooker. As he ran through the greenery he could hear the legions of clubby shoes thundering on the sod, crushing everything in their path... trees, flower beds, policemen, in their relentless march to stomp his drip-dry-suited body into the ground.

Loping as he had not done since childhood, the doctor headed up a pathway toward the lake, bowling over a popsicle truck, baby carriage, kids on bikes, all the while cringing from the murderous banshee wail close at his heels.

How to escape being I. Millered or A. S. Becked to death? To be snapped into eternity by a begirdled, pantyhosed mob gone berserk?

How? How?

Then he saw a rowboat at the edge of the lake being pushed off by a breasty, pleasant-faced young lady in her late twenties. "Quick! Quick! Take me with you!"

"You're mad! I'm going to call the police!" the girl screamed and swung an oar at him.

"Please, please, my dear young woman. I am Dr. Henry Kissingherr."

"A doctor?"

"*Ja.*" He jumped into the boat.

"Jewish?"

"*Ja,* but please hurry. They're gaining on me."

"Am I glad I listened to Momma! She always knew I'd find a Jewish doctor. Let's go."

And she pushed off thirty precious seconds before the rampaging Libbers reached the shore and with sturdy strokes she propelled it into the lake center. "Hi, I'm Sheila Levine, I'm dead and I'm living in New York." Then she thought a second. "Wait, did you say your name was Dr. Henry Kissingherr?"

"*Ja.*"

"Not *the* Kissingherr?"

"*Ja.*"

"Well, you sure look like that face in the Harvard Lampoon, but I don't believe it. Would Dr. Kissingherr be in the middle of Central Park being chased by a gang of angry women? He doesn't waste his time that way. He's too busy with international intrigue and things like that."

"I assure you I am."

"Then prove it. Say something in foreign policy."

Knowing there was no time to waste, the doctor let go. "As insidious as any usage of germ warfare is an attack upon a nation's monetary system, which could cause a drastic imbalance in trade, a debilitation of the currency and ultimately wide-scale unemployment."

"Oh, my God, wide-scale unemployment!" she screamed and began to undo her Jeans East big-cuffed slacks. Before he could conclude his resumé of America's economic woes she was pulling him down to the bottom of the boat into a *Poseidon Adventure* he would never forget. Once out of their sight, the hordes on the shore lost interest in him and they worked off their excess energy by beating up three hardhats.

In the rowboat, the long-suppressed sexual desires of Sheila Levine were unwinding like taffy in a boardwalk candy shop in Atlantic City and for four hours she went through a series of vigorous exercises to be found only in the *Royal Canadian Air Force Manual*. At five o'clock a bone-weary Dr. Kissingherr looked plaintively at the sky and prayed, *"Hurry, Sundown."*

Sated at last, she rowed him back to the shore and they parted with oddly formal handshakes considering all they had experienced in their skin-to-skin wingding.

"In your energetic way, Miss Levine, you may have saved America," he said, bowing to kiss her hand.

"Golly," she answered with a grin. "I think I'm coming back to the lake tomorrow. Who knows who'll be here then? Maybe Erich Segal."

"Here, Miss Levine, a token of my esteem and affection." He pressed a gold-rimmed laminated card into her fingers. "My VIP card to Disneyland, which allows you free access to any attraction on the premises. Except the Pirate's Cave. That's extra, you know."

She nodded. "Of course." And walked out of Dr. Henry Kissingherr's life forever.

His mood underwent a dramatic change. Again Mizz Steinway had nearly ended his life and now it was time to take off the kid gloves, and with any luck, he thought, a spicy gleam in his eye, Glory's blouse, belt, and bikini pants.

At his order the CIA struck. She was taken forcibly from the editorial room of *Mizz* during the last sentence of a total rewrite of a classic novel, soon destined for the Woman's Lib bookstore—the scene where Scarlett said to Rhett, "Frankly, my dear chauvinist pig, I don't give a fuck"—whisked in an unmarked car to a "safe house" on Sutton Place, there to face a nasty-looking Dr. Kissingherr.

"Now we talk about Ronrico, Mizz Steinway."

"No. So what comes next, Kraut?" she said bravely. "The Iron Maiden, the thumbscrews, the rack?" A single bulb swung over her tresses, casting eerie shadows on the white-washed wall.

"Your kind does not yield so readily to physical mistreatment. In fact, you have a secret wish to be tortured for it makes you more of a martyr in your own eyes. What I have for you is infinitely worse."

He snapped his fingers. An agent set up a projector, killed the light and began flashing slides which the CIA, utilizing mockup techniques, had quickly put together.

The first showed her at the keyboard of a Remington Rand typewriter pounding out letters, making coffee for an exec, catering to his every need, then being pinched by same, finally on his lap being fondled like a plaything.

Glory Steinway's mouth began to twitch.

More slides. Glory in a Playboy Bunny outfit. The faces of leering men. Hands clawing at her thighs and buttocks. Everything calculated to perpetuate the subordinate status of women.

More slides. Glory bending over a sink of filthy dishes. A chocolate-smeared brat tugging at the hem of her housedress. Arguing with a high-priced plumber. Sitting among women at a meeting with the banner WOODLAKE ELEMENTARY SCHOOL P.T.A. on a back wall.

Oh, Lordess, is this what this horn-rimmed fiend has in store for me? she thought, a whimper escaping from deep within. A life of shelling peas, standing at checkout counters, her marvelous brain atrophying with each lick of an S & H Green Stamp. "No..." and her hand flew to her throat.

"Tell me about Ronrico."

She clenched her teeth and remained mute.

The slides clicked on... Glory making beds, darning socks, reading *Family Circle* and *Woman's Day,* the premiere event of her life the preparation of a Shake N' Bake chicken dinner.

"I'll never talk... never," but by the convulsions he knew she was close to the breaking point.

He snapped his fingers again and the slide show ceased. "And to share with you this lifetime of domestic bliss on a CIA-operated farm in Nevada from which there is no escape, may I present..."

A door opened.

"The man you will live with the rest of your life."

A scowl on his plump face, a cheap cigar gripped in his yellowed teeth, a beer-bellied man in a bowling shirt, Robert Hall slacks and sneakers who looked horrifyingly like television's leading bigot, lumbered into the room and smirked at Glory. "You're gonna live wit' me..."

She was about to scream when the man growled, "Stifle yourself, dingbat, and fix me my supper." Her granny glasses fell off her face and Glory Steinway pitched forward in a dead faint. A little ammonia under the nose and she was quickly revived.

"I'll talk, for God's sake, I'll talk. But take that... thing away!"

The CIA director patted the doctor on his ample tummy. "Good show, Henry. In my long career in covert operations I've become acquainted with sadistic and brutal interrogations, but I've never seen a masterful job like the one you just did on Miss Mizz over here."

He and the doctor lit victory cigars, found themselves impelled by a desire to root for the Boston Celtics, leaned back and Glory, regaining her poise, put on her granny glasses and unfolded her narrative.

TWENTY-THREE

She had been hard at work laying out *Mizz's* Mother's Day issue whose front cover depicted a woman, serene in a rocking chair, cradling a gigantic Ortho-Novum birth control pill in her arms, when a messenger brought a sealed envelope, insisting that she alone view its contents.

"It was an invitation to attend a conference open to a select few on the isle of Ronrico and it promised a striking new philosophy that would fit into my way of thinking. Inside was a first-class round trip ticket and a number to call for further information. I called," Glory said, "and after listening to the compelling arguments of a man who assured me he had a master plan for changing the world that fit into my political scheme of things, I decided to go. I checked into the El Fidel Hotel, and having a few hours to kill I organized a chambermaids' strike against the sexist management, and then at night attended the most interesting parley of my life. It was an odd bunch in that suite... people from all walks, among them a Chinese, Dr. Ling Ah Ling, Rafer Raper, the pornographer, and Cap'n Amos Lobster, a taciturn old man in an oilslicker, high rubber boots and knitted cap who spoke with a New England twang so salty it could have pickled a lox. And he carried a harpoon."

At this the doctor's owlish eyes flickered with keen interest. "Run a check on Lobster," he scribbled on a pad.

"And there were others," Glory went on, apparently glad to release this secret long festering inside. "There was a retired Air Force Colonel, Jack Cracker, a cracker jack of a pilot in Korea; Dr. Harley Street, a British physician with a gripe against organized medicine, and a ragged mix of mercenaries, some who had fought for causes I espouse, some against. Yet all were mesmerized by the leader, who, speaking to us both collectively and individually, promised a better day if we followed his bold scheme."

"What did the leader look like?"

"We don't know. He wore a Mickey Mouse mask, a touch of ingenuity I found personally appealing. Before I became the radical I am I admit I was a strong fan of Annette Funicello."

"What did he sound like?"

"He attempted to disguise his voice, sometimes slipping into Oxfordian English..."

"A Briton?"

"No, because at other moments in his long, long dissertation where he repeated and repeated his points over and over, hammering his fist on the table, he attempted the accents of a Japanese priest, a Russian industrial plant manager, a Mexican bean picker, even the giggle of Flipper the dolphin. But somehow, despite his vocal tricks, I detected a kind of flat, midwestern nasality creeping into all of it."

"Why did you agree to this plan? Didn't you know there would be violence?"

"Not then," she said ashamed. "I was told there would be kidnappings, your leader's, yours, but no violence."

"You have been duped, Glory. I myself have been the target of assassins, including one in your own apartment, and several people have died," and he briefly reviewed the China, San Francisco, Los Angeles, and New York experiences.

"Again, Glory, why did you follow this man, an individual totally unknown to you?"

"As I said all present were mesmerized, I mizz-merized... you know my thing, Doctor... because that man could talk, oh, God, could he talk... on and on and on... until we were drummed into zombies, eager to do whatever he said."

Dr. Kissingherr paused a moment. Who under the sun could hold an audience for hours with his rhetoric? Who had that kind of nonstop verbosity? Jack Parr? No, that distinguished worthy was working again on television and anyone who had to put together a monologue, photograph lions and tigers and speak to Peggy Cass certainly had no time to mount a cabal. Castro? Wrong on two counts. Though he held enough animosity to spearhead a plot against Yankee imperialists and the forensic ability to ramble on for hours at a clip, he (a) did not have a midwestern accent, and (b) his beard would never have been covered fully by the Mickey Mouse mask.

Then who? Who could speak for hours on end? He had a sudden notion.

"That voice; it intrigues me. Can you recall some of the phrases it used? Did he tell you why he had corralled you all on Ronrico, and what he believed in?"

"Oh, yes," Glory said. "Many times. But now that you mention it, he didn't say the word 'believe' the way you and I do. It came out 'bleeve,' rhyming with 'sleeve.' "

A lightning bolt went off in that mega-brain, sending sixteen synapses scurrying for cover in the canyons of his mind. "One more question, Glory. Did this Mickey Mouse masked man of the midwest," and he chuckled, having spewed out an alliteration the vice president would have given his Jack Nicklaus golf clubs to have originated, "tell you how he felt at the end of the Ronrico conference?"

"He said he was pleased."

"How pleased was he?"

"As a matter of fact, he was pleased as... uh..." and she struggled mentally to remember... "as... as... punch."

TWENTY-FOUR

Kicking the dust of the street off his Florsheim wingtips, Dr. Henry Kissingherr coughed a few more particles out of his parched throat and walked the few yards between the post office and his destination, the YE OLD GOODTIME DRUGSTORE, with its sign, Ice Cream Sodas Made With All the Fixin's, Phosphates Like Gramps Uster Drink 'Em, Warts Removed, Leeches Applied.

The CIA jet had flashed across the continent at 600 miles per hour, bucking the stiff prevailing westerly winds, carrying the doctor, the CIA director and several of his crew-cutted agents.

"The third phone call told me all I needed to know," Dr. Kissingherr commented to the CIA director, but another section of his great mind was sketching out the bargaining points for a rapprochment with Cuba. "Point six, I suggest, would be that we agreed to pay double the rent on Guantanamo and he agrees to send a new Latin dance up north. We haven't had one since the meringue, when he severed relations."

"Henry," the CIA director broke in, "are you sure we've got our man? It sounds insane. If you're wrong we'll be the laughingstock of the world, if there's a world left to laugh."

"*Ja*, I am certain."

"Then we've got to go in there and hit them with everything, make the principals talk, get the Chief back unharmed."

"Barging in would make these conspirators react in an irrational manner and who knows what that would mean? No, I must go in alone."

"Then," and CIA pulled a capsule out of his lapel pocket, "swallow this."

"Why?" the doctor's eyebrows shot up quizzically. "I have no heartburn, no anxiety. I do not require Compoz, that gentle little blue pill."

"It's a gimmick from the lab, a miniaturized beeper device that tells us where you are at all times. Now swallow it. It has a radius of ten miles, but my guys from the Rapid City district will be a damn sight closer than that, I can tell you."

Meanwhile the jet radio was a-crackle, bringing in new data every moment, the profiles on Cap'n Lobster, Dr. Street, Col. Cracker and their known close associates. With each disclosure Dr. Kissingherr was getting the clear picture of their involvement with Mickey Mouse.

And so as he opened the door to the ancient pharmacy, Dr. Kissingherr, even in this tense moment charmed by the tingle of its old-fashioned bell, was certain of what lay within. Since it was 6 P.M. the streets had been rolled up for the night, no pedestrians were to be seen, and hence the establishment was empty.

But there was a dim light in the rear where a man was running a wet rag over the brass soda dispensers and marble-topped counters.

"Come in," boomed a jovial voice. "I've been expecting you." The man pivoted quickly and dropped his rag. The doctor trembled. The pharmacist was wearing a Mickey Mouse mask. "I knew you'd get here eventually, by golly."

His hand fished into the apron and came out with an ugly snub-nosed Smith & Smith revolver, set to cough out its message of death. The other hand ripped off the Disney face.

"Yup, I sure am pleased as punch to see you, Hank," said Humbert Homefree, the United States Senator from Ceresota.

TWENTY-FIVE

"The obvious question: why?" the doctor opened the conversation, uneasy at the gun trained on him but outwardly dispassionate.

"Oh, we have lots of time to talk about that," Homefree chuckled in his happy warrior way. "But first, Hank, how's about a little drink? As you know from my autobiography us Homefrees started out here in South Dakota in the pharmacy business many years ago before moving to Ceresota, where it all began to happen for me. Phosphate for me, Hank. Have the same?"

The Doctor nodded, relieved to see the gun jammed back into the apron while Homefree added the squirt of lemon and the fizzy seltzer to each tall glass, giving the mixture a hearty stir. "Just 'cause I put the old roscoe away, Hank, doesn't mean you should make any foolish moves. Remember, we've still got your man. I know your boys aren't far away, but if they move in... well." He left the sentence unfinished, but the menace in "well" told Dr. Kissingherr reams of information.

"Down the hatch, Hank," the senator chuckled and swallowed his phosphate, giving a satisfied sigh. "Okay, so you want to know why. Drink up, Hank. I'll tell you."

Taking a sip, finding it rather refreshing, the doctor leaned on the counter.

"Hank," the senator said philosophically, "what I have done, kidnapping the president, the vice president, and two aides, could be viewed as a fairly despicable action. But sometimes in order to save the democratic process you've got to destroy it. We found that out in Viet Nam. Hank, I want to be president. It should be as clear to you as it is to me that I am the most qualified man in the country to lead us in these times of peril. Look at my record... mayor, governor, senator, vice president, champion of the working man, friend of business, lover of minorities as long as they don't get too pushy to the majority, friend to the majority as long as they don't get too pushy to the minorities, beloved by blacks, browns, yellows, homosexuals, bisexuals, heterosexuals, alka sexuals—that's a little pharmaceutical joke, Hank. In short, the man all America wants."

"But they didn't want you in a free, duly constituted presidential election; then in your own primary in 1972 they didn't want you again." A snarl curled Homefree's lip, driving off that usual cheerful grin. "That's the trouble with democracy. It's too damn democratic. So, Hank, I spearheaded a little session on Ronrico, which obviously you know about, and power is now within inches of my grasp."

"But you used violence, my dear Senator."

"Hank... go on, feller, drink up..." The doctor downed his phosphate. "If you want to make an omelet you gotta break a few eggs, as they say in Howard Johnson's. A few people had to... uh... go beyond," he said euphemistically, "in order for this plot to succeed. My real target was you, for I knew you were the one man in government capable of figuring this thing out. We missed you in China, in Frisco and in a lot of other places, but now we've come to the end of the line."

"Still beeping," the CIA head said with satisfaction to his aide. "We've got a good fix on Henry and if he can convince Homefree to take him to the Chief we can close in and bust the whole thing wide open."

"May I ask," the doctor said, feeling a slight rumble in his midsection, attributing it to the exotic nature of the lemon phosphate, which he had never tasted before, "How do you intend to grasp this power?"

"Simple, Hank. The president and vice president have agreed, after a little therapy, of course, to sign a document that says roughly: "I, President of the United States, finding myself suddenly incapacitated mentally by the crushing burdens of my office and finding my Vice President also mentally incapacitated, despite the fact he has no burdens of any kind... and in the best interests of the United States hereby turn over the Presidential Seal and its full power to my dear friend, Senator Humbert Homefree of Ceresota, who, although a longtime political foe, is a man I respect because, all party differences aside, he loves America. He should be the man to sit in my place during the PEPPER talks and hold firm to America's interests. Because of my confidence in him, I am asking that the usual sequence of Presidential succession be waived. To all Americans, my love and devotion—The President'."

"How can the succession be waived?" said Dr. Kissingherr, now feeling an even sharper stabbing pain in his intestines.

"Easy, Hank. The secretary of state is a nothing cat, as my constituents in the ghetto would say. You have seen to that by decimating his power with your brilliance. Similarly the other gents in line are unqualified, and so when this document of mine hits the newspapers and television stations, an American public well aware of how urgently needed will be a great leader in Vienna will endorse me in a magnanimous show of bipartisanship." His eyes grew misty, the smile reappeared. "At last, Humbert Homefree, president of the United States."

In his mind he could hear "Hail to the Chief" played by the Marine band, see his own helicopter, his wife redecorating the White House... maybe even changing the name to the Wheat House in honor of his wheat-producing state... himself with Jackie Gleason, Bob Hope and Andy Williams at the annual President Humbert Homefree Golf Classic, posing with the poster child for acne... at Christmas time lighting the annual national Yule tree for the old folks, and lighting up the national marijuana bush for the young generation.

All this Dr. Kissingherr shrewdly read on the face of the determined Ceresota senator. This madman must be stopped, he thought. Now, if only he could con Homefree into taking him to the president and veep, the CIA boys would track that internal beeper and things yet could be righted.

Suddenly the pain hit him hard and Dr. Kissingherr doubled over. What had been in that phosphate? Curare? Cyanide?

Senator Homefree smiled and looked at his watch. "You'll find it right over there, Hank," and pointed at a door marked GENTS. "You know, Hank, after all, I was a high-ranking member of the National Security Council and I know all about those bugs and beepers, one of which is undoubtedly inside you right now and just dying to come out. No curare, Hank, no cyanide, just a double dose of good old magnesia."

But by then the doctor was on his desperate rush, slamming the door behind him.

In a parked car three blocks away a CIA operative said tensely, "He's been in there with Homefree a long time. I wonder if Henry has flushed him out yet."

But unbeknownst to them, the exact opposite had occurred. "Let's move in," the CIA head barked.

"Hey, chief," said a startled agent. "You do a helluva imitation of a German shepherd."

"Knock off the jokes and let's get cracking," his boss snapped, but thought to himself, hey, I didn't know I could bark like a dog. I'll have to do that at my next house party. Beats the hell out of that old lampshade on the head trick.

But when the CIA teams converged upon the drugstore, smashing their way savagely through the plate glass they found nothing... just two empty glasses on the marble counter and a beep-beep-beep coming from the john. Their quarry and his prestigious prisoner were gone.

TWENTY-SIX

Manacled, a blindfold over his prominent nose and owlish eyes, the presidential agent felt the jouncing of the van over the rough trail. At the wheel was Senator Homefree, who, well aware of the CIA cordon, had led his captive through a passageway directly into the next-door edifice, the South Dakota School of Mines, built directly over the old El Balagoola Zinc Mine which had enriched Rapid City in the middle of the nineteenth century. Ultimately the zinc vein had run out and now there was scarcely enough for a Mason jar bottle cap. It was through these abandoned, clammy tunnels that the senator had reached his vehicle located well outside of the security perimeter.

In twenty minutes the van pulled into the hippie commune. Homefree led his prisoner past the residents who were hard at work at their most recent, rather daring project, trying to make a complete human being out of macrame. "If we can bring it to life," said one bearded communalist, whose name happened to be Viktor Frankenstein, "we can even equal the power of God."

"God? What has She got to do with it?" cried one of the female members, working her strings into an approximation of the nervous system.

"Hey," laughed another resident. "This commune is getting freakier all the time. Now we got a dude who wants to look like Henry Kissingherr. Well, baby," he said to the doctor, "whatever turns you on..."

In the lodge house Dr. Kissingherr, prodded by the point of the senator's Smith & Smith, shook with revulsion. There in a corner, guarded by several mean-faced individuals, was his commander in chief, those usually penetrating eyes now rolling about in a state of stupor. He mumbled, "Hi, Henry, wanna try some great grass? They grow it here. And, hey, did you get my memo compelling the Pentagon to cut forty-five percent of its budget for new military hardware?"

My God, the doctor thought, is he out of it!

In the next cot was the vice president. "Oh, I am so deeply dismayed about this constant condition of captivity during which my mobility to meander has been cruelly curtailed by the inhuman imprisonment of my bodily being by these..."

A doctor cut off what could have meant another three hours of alliterations with a fast injection that sent the vice president into a nod immediately.

"Perhaps, Hank, you should meet the boys," Homefree said in his folksy tone. "My friend, the British surgeon, Dr. Harley Street."

"Pleased to meet you, old chap," the medico piped up.

"Dr. Street," said Senator Homefree, "is a brilliant man of medicine, far ahead of his time, but as is so often the case he was rejected by his conservative colleagues."

"Damned fools," the physician spat in sudden ire. "I had a smashing plan to help mankind by curing the common headache, but the greedy swine fought me at every turn, virtually drummed me out of the medical association."

"But is the common headache not already curable by aspirin?" Dr. Kissingherr asked.

"Yes," sneered Dr. Street, "but how much aspirin and how often? I'll tell you, billions and billions of bottles a year.

"Yes, those doctor blighters and their bloodsucking kin in the drug industry are making a fortune. Is it any wonder they ridiculed and tried to stop the Dr. Harley Street lifetime aspirin? Just one, taken at an early age, gives you enough time-release medicine to fight this scourge from cradle to grave. Can you imagine," Dr. Street said, "a medical profession where a doctor is unable to stay to a suffering patient in the wee hours, 'Take two aspirins and call me in the morning'? That phrase alone is the backbone of organized medicine."

"You can do that with just one aspirin?"

"Yes. This one." From his inside pocket Dr. Street yanked out a white circular object that the Powerkraut first took to be a Frisbee or a Lennox china dinnerplate.

"How do you swallow a pill that immense?"

"Slowly and with a lot of water," the physician conceded. "But this whole conversation is giving me a splitting headache." He took a huge bite out of the disc. "I have a number five aspirin that comes with pepperoni and mushrooms and a number six with everything." His eyes widened.

Dr. Kissingherr's interest was waning in the face of Dr. Street's patent medicine madness. His eyes and nose strayed to the next conspirator, the latter sense assailed by the powerful essence of fish. "And you," he said to the man whose face was as weatherbeaten as his oilslicker, the man whose gnarled fingers clutched a harpoon, "you would be Cap'n Amos Lobster and I know your motivation. You, sir, are the leader of a disgruntled faction of New Bedford fishermen who have been carping— forgive my seafood sally— against what you believe to be your government's weakness in facing up to the incursion of Russian trawlers off your beloved coast."

"Hank, you've been doing your homework," the senator chuckled.

"Them damn Russkies, takin' our fish from our waters and the baked beans from our kids' bellies. This here president of your'n warn't doin' a damn thing, so ol' Amos decided we needed a change."

"You are famous, indeed, as the harpoonist who has never missed, Cap'n Lobster."

"Eh-yeah, I'm the gent who got Moby Dick the hard way. I flung my harpoon through the main window of the New Bedford library spearin' Herman Melville's novel right in the bindin'. So, bub, twarn't no big thing for me to put my extra-special harpoon through that ol' copter without hurtin' no one." And having made what amounted to a Rotary Club speech for him, the untalkative Lobster strolled out of the lodge, palpably bored with the entire proceedings.

Incredible, the doctor thought, then turned to a short-haired stocky man in a pilot's uniform with enough fruit salad on the lapel to make Del Monte envious. "And it is a pleasure to meet you, Col. Jack Cracker, you who no doubt flew the Goodtire blimp. But you who swore military allegiance, you who compiled an ace's record in Korea... why?"

"Because," and the gung ho airman paused to spray a dash of Reddi-Wip on his fruit salad, "this country has let its air force go to pot, in more ways than one. We keep cutting back when any damn fool knows we need thousands and thousands of new bombers, fighters, interceptors to keep the Commies at bay. In fact, we should see to it that anything with wings is up there for America. Commercial jets, small private planes... we should be training eagles to carry napalm, butterflies with tiny nuclear warheads to crash kamikazi style into enemy ships, even Jonathan Livingston Seagull should cut out that philosophy shit and carry heat-seeking missiles. Air power, that's the ticket, and this administration is a mess of pusillanimous pussyfooters!"

With that alliteration the vice president stirred and was about to counterpunch with one of his own, but a glance from Homefree sent Dr. Street back with the needle and the Greek slid back into limbo.

"The ol' doc here knows me," grinned the giant Rafer Raper. "You didn't make a very good pornographer, kraut. I smelled you out fast. I have a noncocaine nostril set aside for that purpose."

"And you, Herr Raper, doubtless have been told if you cooperate with the president-to-be that pornography will be legalized."

"More than that, baby," Raper said. "My dear senator, he's gonna put me in charge of a new network, Pornographic Erotic Television—PET, as it'll be known in your *TV Guide.* I gonna be the Sarnoff of Sex, the Paley of Pussy. All my flicks gonna run on pay television and I gonna make more bread than Wonder."

"So greed is your motivation, is it not so?"

"No, baby. I doin' it for the betterment of my people. With the proceeds I'm gonna have Watts and Harlem moved to Waikiki Beach."

The president stirred, muttered, "Put people on welfare rolls, not payrolls," then lapsed back into his dreamy state.

Oy gevald, his advisor moaned. He's really out of it.

Senator Homefree smiled confidentally. "So you see, Hank, when you've been around the way I have all these years you can spot these pockets of discontent just waiting to be exploited. The left wing, the right wing..."

"He understands!" Col. Cracker jumped in excitedly. "Wings, that's what we need, wings! Fruit flies who can be spies, sparrows trained to kill, bobolinks, pigeons," and he rattled off the entire Audubon Society index until the senator cooled him down with a few calming words.

"Just a few key people, Hank, that's all it needed. And in twenty-four hours, I, Humbert Homefree, Senator of Ceresota, will be the commander in chief. Come along, Hank, I want you all to see something."

All the captives were herded into the van, the president saying from time to time that he thought Timothy Leary would be a splendid choice for secretary of agriculture. They jolted along in relative silence, Homefree at the wheel, a great sunburst of a smile spreading his lips, his eyes messianic, his lips crooning "This land is my land."

About a half-hour out of the commune Dr. Kissingherr heard the gears grinding as the vehicle struggled on an upgrade. Then the ignition was cut and the senator leaned over the backseat. "We're here, gents. Come take a look."

The president, vice president, and the doctor were taken into the early dawn, blinking their eyes at the slowly rising ball of fire peeping over the Black Hills.

"No funny stuff, Herr Doktor," said Rafer Raper, the automatic in his ham-hock of a hand looking like a toy.

"Behold," said Senator Homefree, pointing a finger that sent Col. Cracker, Cap'n Lobster and Dr. Street into action. They moved toward the top of a towering bluff over which had been draped strangely a great section of black velvet cloth. "Heave to, maties," Cap'n Lobster grunted, as though he were on the deck of a whaler, and the three men sweating and cursing tugged at the cloth until after some minutes they pulled it up to the cliff top.

"My God!" cried Dr. Henry Kissingherr. "It's unbelievable." For now he knew where they had been taken. They stood atop the Mount Rushmore Memorial, the home of those great and solemn faces... indeed, on the very head of George Washington.

And there at the left of the Father of His Country, newly etched in granite it stood, grinning over the valley.

The face of Senator Humbert Homefree of Ceresota!

TWENTY-SEVEN

In the Great Hall of the Chateau Briand, the only castle in Europe made entirely of meat, the workmen were putting everything in readiness for the first plenary session of the Congress of Vienna. The full delegations from Russia, China, Japan, Britain, and France were all in town by now, but there was one glaring exception, the U.S.A., with only its second-level echelon checked into the Strauss Hilton, causing even deeper anxiety among the conferees. Where was the president? His schedule had called for him to be in Vienna twenty-four hours before PEPPER opened for the usual ceremonial folderol, a state dinner with the leader of the host country, a visit to the opera for a new production of Wagner's "Ring" trilogy (sponsored aptly enough by Tiffany's), and the opening of Vienna's first McDonald's.

His absence sent shock waves reverberating throughout the diplomatic community, the Communist bloc in particular looking more grim and resigned with each passing hour. And in dozens of unholy places beneath the earth the missiles waited for their coded commands.

TWENTY-EIGHT

"Who did this... this desecration of a national treasure?"

"Why, Hank," said Homefree. "I did it. ol' Humby, that's who. For a year I came here night after night with chisels, hammers, explosives. Working with a scale model of my own face I let myself down over the cliff by ropes on pulleys and jes' kept workin' away like the indefatigible beaver I am. Not bad for a li'l ol' pharmacist, right?"

The doctor seemed stunned. "You did this? With all the duties incumbent upon you as a United States Senator?"

"Hank, I have reached a phase of my physical development in which I am able to go virtually without sleep. I am a driven man and such men need no slumber. Of course, I was able to catch a little catnap now and then on the Senate floor, 'cause there nobody can tell whether you're awake or not. So most of the time I was on my private jet coming out here, chipping away at night, whipping my scheme into shape, contacting my conspirators with portable telephonic equipment... just doing the million and one things of which I am capable, keeping all the balls bouncing in the air at the same time. And now I shall have this memorial to forever remind my countrymen of the greatest president ever to sit in the Oval Room."

"I suppose then it is time for our final reckoning, Senator."

Homefree thought hard for a moment. "Yes, Hank. You're too dangerous to let live. But I have a last-ditch proposition for you. I could use your brains at Vienna, in fact all during my next two administrations. And, Hank, here's a little enticement for you. If you show up at Vienna as my right hand man at the PEPPER talks, your presence will do much to legitimize mine. With the great Kissingherr at my side, the initial furore will soon die down, stability will return and," he pointed to the glassy-eyed president and vice president, "these people will soon be lost in the backwater of history. We'll have them committed to a nice rest home where they can watch Superbowl reruns until it's time for their Social Security. And here's something else, Hank. If I can't change the two-term law and am forced to step down in 1981, you, Hank, will be my personal choice for president. Think of it... Henry Kissingherr, the first Jewish president of the good ol' USA. All you gotta do is forsake your allegiance to this man and climb aboard my team. Think fast, Hank. You got ten seconds."

Several quick images flashed through that mega-brain during Homefree's slow, deliberate countdown. The sacred words of the Kaddish, the Jewish prayer for the dead... the faces of his loved ones... a cool day under the leafy green foliage at Harvard... a huge plate of lox, eggs and onions (odd what goes through the mind at a moment like this, he thought)... a sensible scenario for ending the miseries in Northern Ireland (that's more like it, he thought)... and then he drew himself up and said with a quiet grandeur, *"Nein."*

"I'm only up to eight, Hank," corrected the senator.

"Nein means no in German."

"Then die, Hank, die," and the senator motioned to Lobster, whose eyes became steely slits measuring their target.

And Henry Kissingherr, knowing that he was but a second or two away from being impaled like a German-Jewish whale (a much bigger target than a German-Jewish porcupine), searched for that one hidden brain cell that could save him. And then an alpha wave responded to his urging. He, who had dedicated his life to bringing together men of diverse opinions, would reverse the process.

"Auf weidersehen, Cap'n Lobster, and I sincerely hope you enjoy watching all those fine, clean-hearted children of your beloved Yankee heritage being poisoned hour by hour by the filmic production of Herr Raper here."

"What do you mean poisoning our kids? This here colored man ain't nothin' but a photographer. What's wrong with that?"

"No, no, my dear Captain. He is a pornographer, quite a difference. He produces filthy films."

"Shut up," Raper growled.

"No, go on, mate," Cap'n Lobster said. "You mean like them dirty movies of people spawning?"

"Precisely."

"Dammit," the old New Englander spun toward Homefree. "You didn't tell me nothin' about that stuff. Maybe you're lyin' about savin' them fish too."

"But, Amos, old friend," the senator said, putting an arm around the oilslicker, finding the captain's shoulders stiffening.

"Well, fuck you and your fuckin' fish, you honkey harpoon freak," roared Raper. "Sure, I make dirty films and so what?"

"Gentlemen, you're both getting rather agitated needlessly," interrupted Dr. Street. "A bite of my aspirin, perhaps?"

"Screw you and your aspirin, you limey clown," Raper said. "When I get a headache, I'll take Excedrin."

"Excedrin?" The word was like waving a red flag in front of a bull. And Dr. Street, despite his slender size, rushed Raper, swinging his huge nibbled aspirin like a machete.

When Raper landed a smashing blow that flattened the Briton like a pancake, it set off the boiling anger in Cap'n Lobster who switched positions like a cat and sent his instrument whizzing at the black giant. It went through sickeningly, Raper screamed and the dream of Pornocat Productions dominating television was over. The man who pushed phallic penetrations had died fittingly in a similar manner.

"What have you done, you mad New England chowderhead?" screamed Homefree. "You've killed the wrong man."

"Well, I ain't lettin' no damn dirty movie maker..." but his twang was stilled forever when Col. Jack Cracker, enraged at the sudden turn of events that threatened to strip him of his longed-for aerial armadas that would darken the sun like a plague of locusts, emptied his entire clip of bullets into the center of that oilslicker and the old whaler went to Davy Jones's locker.

Now Kissingherr knew what he must do to save his skin. He saw the impaled Raper, who had been driven back by the force of the thrust between two pine trees, and the long coil of rope that had dropped out of the dead harpoonist's hand. Snatching that serpentine circle, he flung it over the side and began to clamber down as fast as his plump physique would allow.

"Stop him!" Homefree shouted at Colonel Cracker. "Climb down after him, get him!"

"Climb hell," said the airman. "I don't have to climb. I can fly down to him and peck him to death. I have wings!"

With dismay the senator realized quickly that his co-conspirator had overidentified with his winged philosophy. He paled to watch Colonel Cracker rev up his arms and take a flying leap off the top of Washington's head with a shout of, "Icarus, you were right! Man can fly!"

There was a terrible crunch as Cracker's body hit the brow of the first president, then fell far out of sight.

Kissingherr, on the rope, felt the wind whipping him against Washington's face and then past it toward the aristocratic nose of Jefferson.

"My God," Washington whispered to the writer of the Declaration of Independence. "We're being invaded by madmen."

"What are you complaining about?" Jefferson retorted. "One of them is climbing on me." And it was true, for the doctor had sought refuge from Homefree, now also climbing down on the rope, his eyes ablaze with frustration, firing wildly.

Where was that damn kraut? he snarled. Grasping the rope with his left hand, his Smith & Smith in his right hand, he paused in his descent to listen for his quarry.

"Achoo!" The sneeze echoed throughout the valley and automatically Homefree said, "*Gezuntheit,* Tom Jefferson," and he continued raking those questing eyes over the statues. Wait, he told himself, statues don't sneeze. It's that damn Kissingherr. He's hiding in Tom's dusty old nose. "Come out, Hank! It's all over."

The doctor could see the shadow of the approaching senator's body stealing over the face of Jefferson and realized he could no longer stay put. He moved from his recess in the nostril and froze. There was the grinning face of Homefree, that frightening pistol pointed at his head. "This is it, Hank!" and the fingers tightened, but the doctor sprang back into the darkness and the bullet whizzed by harmlessly, bouncing throughout the nasal cavity.

"Oh, Lord," Jefferson called out. "My sinus is killing me."

"Oh, bully, bully!" cried Teddy Roosevelt. "I haven't had so much excitement since I founded the Bull Moose party."

Crouching inside the darkened nose, Dr. Kissingherr thought, this indeed is it. His hands scrabbled around for some sort of weapon, finding only dust caused by the drilling of the faces.

And something else. A section of rope hooked into the granite by a mountain climber's piton, possibly abandoned there by a careless workman who under Borglum's guidance had worked on the face. There was a great length of it, but how old was it? How many years had it been exposed to wind, rain, and sun? Was it corroded? Would it hold? Another shot whistled into the cavern and Henry Kissingherr found himself with but one option. He would have to take the chance. Scooping up a handful of powdery granite he flung it desperately into the entrance of the nostril, catching Homefree flush in his face, and when he saw the Ceresotan choking and blinded he grabbed the old rope and swung over the valley, wrenching the senator's gun from his hand in a swift flowing motion as he passed his enemy.

Now the two men were like clock pendulums swinging hundreds of feet, from Washington to Lincoln, occasionally brushing in midair, landing feeble blows, two middle-aged paunchy men, neither possessing even the punching power of Don Knotts.

And so they swung back and forth, fatigued to the bone, hurling aimless imprecations at each other, so arm-weary now that it seemed only a matter of time that either or both would plummet to the valley below. Suddenly, Dr. Kissingherr felt a sensation of being pulled upward. He looked at the top of Jefferson's nose to see the CIA chief and his contingent yanking and calling out, "Hold on, Doctor, hold on..." and blessedly he was in their arms, panting a prayer of thanks, and then there was only poor Humbert Homefree swaying back and forth crying out in a pitiful whimper, "I am the president... I am the president... I am the president...."

TWENTY-NINE

The strains of the minuet fell softly upon the ears of the world's leaders, now bedecked in powdered wigs, ornate greatcoats and tight-fitting satin breeches, the same garb that had been worn in the historic Congress of Vienna One. Waiters bustled to the great burnished table with Dom Perignon champagne which the stocky Russians, bulging in their skin-tight finery, were belting down like cheap vodka. Though there was a continuous round of boisterous toasting, cries of "peace and friendship," somehow there was a hollowness in all of it as their eyes kept straying toward the unoccupied American chairs. The rumors of yesterday had magnified tenfold and there were all kinds of dire speculations: revolution in America, possible cracking apart of the NATO alliance, troops massed on all borders and not even the secretary of state who had come in the advance party could allay them, although he was for the first time enjoying his role as top dog in the absence of his commander in chief and that damn Powerkraut.

Despite the music, the drinks, and the laughter which grew shriller, the ticking away of the minutes sounded like great drums of doom thundering in the hearts of the potentates. They knew that in the silos the faces of the missilemen were ashen as they picked up their keys to open the combinations, that bombers were nearing their fail-safe points awaiting only the word "go," that subs were ghosting near each other's coasts and that if the acknowledged top man of the world failed to appear...

A herald lifted an ancient elongated trumpet to his lips but so rattled was he by the tension hanging over the Great Hall that instead of hitting a fanfare he went right into the famous Harry James trumpet solo of "You Made Me Love You" and before he was halted by a black look three Russians asked three Chinese if they'd care to dance and they did, fox-trotting romantically cheek-to-cheek, the Russians dipping elegantly. Then the fanfare was hit.

"Gentlemen," said the Austrian leader. "The Congress of Vienna Two has begun."

They filed into the conference room, each with his aides, and seated themselves, again looking with horror at the unfilled seat with the nameplate, "President of the United States." When they saw that lonely chair the Russians and Chinese realized it was hopeless. They whispered frantic instructions to their military aides who got up like automatons and began a march toward the massive oaken door. Suddenly there was a pounding on the floor by a page driving his staff and a joyous cry, "Gentlemen, the president of the United States!"

The Communist military men stopped in their tracks. Past them marched Dr. Kissingherr, wearing a blindingly white wig and black beauty spot on his chin; the vice president in an Arnold Palmer golfing outfit (his faux pas was overlooked as par for the course for him) and in the middle, his high-heeled shoes with their rows of diamond buckles glinting in the chandelier light, was the leader of the Free World.

"It could yet be a trick," the Russian ambassador told his chairman. "They have used impressionists before." And the Chinese were whispering the same thought amongst themselves.

"My fellow world leaders," the late arrival said. "It sure is great to face a Congress that isn't controlled by the Democrats... hah, hah, hah," and he punched out his big joke with that nervous half-cough, half-laugh.

"That's the worst joke I've ever heard," grunted the Russian leader. "That *is* the real president of the United States."

"It's got to be," said the Peking foreign minister. "He's only been here ten seconds and his beard is growing. Look, there's a Norelco in his hand..."

And the Congress of Vienna Two convened in an atmosphere of tranquility, the red-alert lights all over the world snuffed out by sweet sanity.

THIRTY

Three weeks later in the Rose Garden, under a warm Washington sun, the president stood with Senator Humbert Homefree of Ceresota in front of a battery of TV cameras and microphones.

"Senator, in appointing you ambassador to Raftlandia, that newly admitted member of the family of nations, which although it is composed of only five Portugese sailors on a wooden raft, bids fair to become a vital factor in the days to come, I know I am sending a man to the South Pacific who will do the very best for America." The crowd applauded and the senator smiled. "We have already," the president went on, "recognized Raftlandia, sent her extra lumber and nails so that she may keep growing and now in her honor the Marine band will play her new Burt Bacharach anthem, 'Raindrops Keep Falling On My Raft.' "

"Are you sure this is the most important job around?" the Senator, who seemed less ebullient than usual, asked in a pleading voice.

"Absolutely, Humby. We need you out there. God knows how we need you out there," and he had the good taste not to say, "far from here." The anthem was rendered and the ceremony broke up.

It had been Henry's idea. "My president," he had said in his low, thrilling voice, "the world must never know that America was threatened by an internal takeover. Send Homefree to the most obscure place you can think of and let him play out the string there."

And Henry's common sense and charitable instincts had prevailed in the case of the remaining plotters. Dr. Street had been sent to a resthome in England where he would be allowed to construct aspirins as big as he wanted to, one of which had been purchased by the city of Dallas as a stadium to complete with Houston's, the former's to be known as the Aspirindome. Glory, whose role had been motivated at least by lofty aims, was given merely a stiff reprimand, told to remain silent and made to clean up the White House on Tuesdays and Thursdays. The mad Dr. Ling Ah Ling was quietly turned over to the Chinese who forced him to take up those deadly acupuncture needles and knit an entirely new Burma Road in wool, a project sure to keep him occupied for many years.

And a Miss Hepzibah Coddingfeather was given a secret citation for her sharp eyes. It was she, sneaking back from a camper after a little swinging of her own, who had noticed the swinging of the figures on the great faces, notified the forest rangers who in turn had notified the CIA and hence the rescue of the doctor, the president and the veep and the freeing of the bound codecarrier and Marine pilot from their commune lodge.

Now it was four weeks later and Dr. Henry Kissingherr stood at the poolside of Jill St. James, observing with keenness those supple limbs, flaming hair and sparkling eyes.

"Well, Henry," she said, "long time no see. What did you do? Save the world from doom in the last few weeks?"

"Not exactly," he said in his modest way. "But I have learned something about the aspirations of people from different minority groups, their longings, their goals and that my president and I must humanize our personal philosophies to take these things into account."

"Oh, how dreadfully interesting," she said, barely stifling a yawn. He moved to kiss her but ran into stony lips. And he realized in that gelid moment that Jill St. James was only intrigued by the trappings of power, "the ultimate aphrodisiac," as he had once termed it. Yes, Jill was a power groupie, as much as some young ladies were Mick Jagger rock groupies or drag race groupies. Then he would give her a dose of power. Now!

She was still rigid in his arms, when he said lightly, "Oh, did I tell you what the Chinese chairman told me about the Quemoy and Matsu incident of the 1960s?"

"Oh, God... Quemoy, Matsu!" she said hoarsely and began to unfasten her robe.

"As you know the constant shelling by the Chinese Communists of these Chiang-controlled islands might have precipitated a major conflict in the Far East."

"Oh, constant shelling!" and her fingers flew to his regimental tie, slipping off the Windsor knot, unbuttoning his Van Heusen. "Major conflict... oh, say it again!"

Henry's methodical voice droned on, but by then her monokini, his drip-dry suit were in an untidy pile by the chaise and all that could be heard issuing from that fusion, hotter than any caused by a nuclear reactor, were the words: "Oh, Henry... Oh, Henry... Oh-h-h-h-Hen-n-n-reeeeeeeeeeeee!"

* * * * * *

www.ingramcontent.com/pod-product-compliance
Lightning Source LLC
Chambersburg PA
CBHW022035170626
46808CB00003B/1203